Knights: Reign of Hellfire

Adam D. Levine

iUniverse, Inc.
New York   Bloomington

Copyright © 2009 by Adam D. Levine

All rights reserved. No part of this book may be used or reproduced by any means, graphic, electronic, or mechanical, including photocopying, recording, taping or by any information storage retrieval system without the written permission of the publisher except in the case of brief quotations embodied in critical articles and reviews.

iUniverse books may be ordered through booksellers or by contacting:

iUniverse
1663 Liberty Drive
Bloomington, IN 47403
www.iuniverse.com
1-800-Authors (1-800-288-4677)

Because of the dynamic nature of the Internet, any Web addresses or links contained in this book may have changed since publication and may no longer be valid. The views expressed in this work are solely those of the author and do not necessarily reflect the views of the publisher, and the publisher hereby disclaims any responsibility for them.

ISBN: 978-1-4401-7618-0 (sc)
ISBN: 978-1-4401-7614-2 (hc)
ISBN: 978-1-4401-7615-9 (ebook)

Printed in the United States of America

iUniverse rev. date: 05/04/2010

For Josh and Jordan.

Without a doubt, you were my inspiration for this story.

Chapter 1

A New Adventure

"OK, Dan, you're up!"

Daniel Rubin walked a few steps, then turned and faced the wall. He was facing away from everyone in the room but was still told to close his eyes. He heard a faint rustle behind him as people shifted their weight or pointed at one another. He could have heard more if he wanted to, but he was content with waiting. After a few seconds he was asked to turn around. He opened his eyes and looked out into the room.

He was looking lengthwise down a long room, the floor of which was covered with mats. On either side of the room there was a row of black belts holding wooden knives, all facing the center of the room. While his back was turned three attackers had been chosen. Daniel would have to walk in between the two rows of black belts, and as he walked past the attackers they would come at him with the wooden knives. He would have to defend himself cleanly, without hurting the other person, which is the trademark of Ju-Jitsu, the martial art that he studied.

Before he moved, he looked out at the other people in the room. They were of various ages and sizes, ranging from thirteen years old and up, from small and light to large and muscular. They were all wearing black *hakamas* over their pants, the ancient formal wear of the samurai worn by practitioners of Japanese martial arts on formal occasions. With their *hakamas* they wore thick white tops traditionally worn by judo players, thus the name "judo top." Every Thursday was black belts only at the dojo, or martial arts school, and they all had to dress formally.

Daniel was dressed the same way, and looked at ease in his formal wear. Daniel was not tall, about average height. He wore his black hair short but spiked up, and his light green eyes shone as the light danced off them. He had a muscular build, though when he wore a shirt it was difficult to tell. He was nineteen years old and a third degree black belt and had been training in the martial arts for fourteen years. Daniel began to walk through what he referred to as "the pipe."

He walked warily, knowing that at any moment he would have to defend himself against the other skilled people in the room. While the wooden knives would not necessarily break skin, they would strike hard enough to leave a large and painful bruise, so Daniel had to be on his guard. He passed four black belts, and then was attacked fiercely. The attacker was Jacob Raines, his longtime best friend. Jake was taller than Daniel, and he had a similar build to Daniel. He wore his brown haircut very close, slightly longer on top than on the side, in a military haircut. Jake was doing ROTC, or the Reserve Officer Training Corps, in order to go into the Marines right after college. His brown eyes were deep and seemed to possess a knowledge that never made it to the surface. He was also a third degree black belt; in fact, he and Daniel had tested for their belts on the same day.

Jake attacked by bringing the knife down in an overhead swing, straight for Daniel's forehead. Daniel sidestepped the attack, threw a punch past Jake's face and then turned under the arm twice, sending Jake flat on his back. Daniel took the knife and laid it on the floor out of Jake's reach, then kept walking.

The next attacker was Gabriel Rubin, Daniel's brother. He was very similar to Daniel in appearance, had the same colored eyes, wore his hair the same way, and was the same height as his brother. People often thought they were twins, while in fact Daniel was five years older. Gabe was a second degree black belt, the youngest in his dojo's history by two days.

Gabe attacked his brother by lunging straight for his chest with the tip of the knife. Daniel sidestepped and brought his hand up in case of a second attack. Then he grabbed Gabe's wrist and threw a kick past his ribs. He turned Gabe's palm toward the floor and pressed, sending Gabe flat on his back. He moved the knife and walked on.

The final attacker was Robert Raines, his brother's best friend and his best friend's brother. Robert was exactly Gabe's age, only two days older. He had tested for his second degree black belt the same day as Gabe, making him the second youngest in dojo history by two days. Robert was almost Jake's height, although other than that the two did not look like brothers. Robert wore his black hair longer than Jake, though still not past the tip of his ears. Although he was almost as tall as Jake and still muscular for his age, Robert had a thinner frame than his older brother. But if there was any doubt of his relation with Jake it disappeared once you looked into his eyes; they were the same deep, rich brown.

He attacked with an upward swing, meant to cut into his victim's belly. Daniel blocked, and then threw a quick back-fist that stopped a quarter inch in front of Robert's face. He quickly put Robert on his back like he had the others. When done full force the moves could break bones, dislocate joints, or even render an opponent unconscious. But full force was rarely necessary; the mere performance of the techniques could temporarily incapacitate the attacker. And, since this was practice, the attacks were much lighter than they would be in combat, and both sparring partners knew how to avoid the injuries. When Robert hit the floor Daniel knew that he was finished, so he faced the room of black belts. His sensei, or teacher, was standing at their head. Daniel brought his feet together and straightened his back. Then he placed his hands on his legs where they met the torso and bowed low. In return his sensei bowed his head. Daniel turned to his three attackers, now all back on their feet, and bowed to them. They bowed back.

The class lined up, facing the front of the room. Daniel and Jake, the two highest ranking students, stood at the front of the first line, with all of the lower ranking students either falling in line next to them or forming their own lines behind the first. They all bowed, saying *"Arigato, Sensei."* This was a thanks to all those who had taught them something throughout their lives. It signified that all are students, and that learning is an integral part of life that never ends. After this they went into the dressing rooms.

"Whoa, Dan, go a little easier next time!" said Robert. "I thought you were gonna rip my shoulder out of the socket!"

Jake grabbed his little brother and put him in a headlock. "Yeah, Dan, twig-boy over here can't handle the pain! I'm surprised he didn't just snap in half!"

"Jake, come on, let me go, your armpit stinks," Robert said, laughing in spite of his hairy situation.

Gabe decided to help out his best friend, and pinched Jake in a very sensitive spot behind the arm. It worked, and Jake released Robert.

"Don't pick on him, you know he's too scrawny to fight back," said Gabe, laughing.

Daniel silently snuck up behind Gabe, grabbed the elastic on the jock strap that was sticking up out of Gabe's pants, and pulled it back. "Yeah, we should pick on people our own size," Daniel said as he released the elastic, which snapped back and cracked against Gabe's lower back.

They finished changing and went out front to the waiting room. They threw their bags on the floor and sat down in some of the chairs. The first person to walk up to them was their friend, Ryan Reilly. He was shorter than Daniel, and had light brown hair with crystal blue eyes. He was a year younger than Daniel, and a year and a half younger than Jake. He was not as muscular as Daniel or Jake, though he was not scrawny. And he was still an outstanding martial artist.

"Hey, guys. Dan, Jake, do you guys have to leave?" Ryan asked.

"Yeah, buddy, we do," said Jake. "But we'll be back in a few months."

"It's just not the same around here without you guys," Ryan said.

"That means a lot," Daniel said. "Why don't you come and visit us, though? I mean, the three of us hanging out in Paris? That'd be awesome."

"Yeah, that would be cool," Ryan said, smiling. "OK, have a great trip; see you when you get back."

With that he shook both of their hands and walked out.

"I'll never understand him," Jake said, shaking his head.

"Yeah, you gotta love him," Daniel said. "Anyway, I'm guessing we're going to be waiting for our moms for a while, so why don't we say goodbye to Sensei?"

"Good idea," said Jake.

When they walked into the office, they saw their sensei sitting at the desk getting ready to close up for the night. They had known him since they were five years old, and he had been like an uncle to them. They had a great deal of respect for him and, though they were his best students, they knew there was still a great deal that they could learn from him. He stood up as he saw them come in.

"Stay out of trouble," he said, hugging them both. "Have a great time, and I'll see you both when you come back."

Almost as one they replied: "Yes, Sensei."

They walked out, and found their mothers there. Lillian Rubin stood waiting for them when they walked out. She had the same features as her sons, but they were soft and beautiful. Jake's mother Marie was waiting next to Lillian. Both were black belts, having followed in the footsteps of their sons. Both were tough, but as mothers, none better could be found. The two families walked out the door together, parted ways and then prepared for the short ride home.

A few minutes later the Rubins walked through their front door and heard the scurry of clawed feet on their tile floor. It was their dog, Roxy. Roxy was a bearded collie, a long-haired black dog with white spots. She was also a champion show dog. Excited to see her mother and her brothers, and forgetting that she was not a small dog, she leaped up to greet them. Gabe, first through the door, was nearly knocked down as she pounced on him. They hugged the dog hello, and then proceeded through the kitchen into the den.

There they saw the youngest of the Rubin brothers, Shane, on the couch watching TV. Shane was still wearing Ju-Jitsu clothes, having gone right before the others for the advanced kid's class. At nine years old, he was the youngest black belt in the dojo. He was small, even for his age. He had lighter hair than his brothers, and brown eyes. He was quite handsome, but because of his size he was most often referred to as "cute." He hated being called cute. He was most noted, however, for a smile that could brighten a room, and a laugh that could bring out the sun on a cloudy day.

Next to Shane on the couch was their father, Ken. Ken was nearly ten years older than his wife, and his gray hair showed only the slightest hints of the reddish brown that it had been. His gray beard showed even less of its original color. But underneath, his face was exactly the same as Shane's. He had the same brown eyes, and the same bright smile that could lift any spirit. Daniel and Gabe brought their food into the den and plopped themselves down onto the couch. Most nights they all ate dinner together, but on Thursday nights whoever went to the dojo ate whenever he got home. They would generally all sit together anyway.

After dinner Daniel laid down on his own bed for a while, just staring at the ceiling. He had never had an experience like the one he was about to have, and he was nervous. It was there that his parents found him. They walked in and sat on the edge of his bed, and he sat up next to them.

"So, you nervous?" Lillian asked.

"No, not really," he lied, but knew that she saw through it.

"Well look, you are going to have a *great* time," Lillian said. "Studying abroad while in college is a great experience. And remember, we're just a phone call away; you can call us any time you want."

"Absolutely," said Ken. "Day or night."

"Thanks, guys," Daniel said. "I just don't know if I can do it."

"Why not?" Lillian asked. "You've faced challenges before. You're a black belt, you've done harder things."

"Yeah, but this is going to be the biggest one yet," Daniel answered.

"Well, of course it's going to be the biggest you've ever faced," Lillian said, smiling. "If it wasn't, it wouldn't be a challenge at all."

"Yeah, you're right," Daniel smiled. "But what if I can't do this?"

"Then so what?" said Ken. "At least you gave it a shot. And I know you; I've known you your whole life. I've watched you grow up into an incredible young man. And I know that you can do anything you set your mind to. I know you can do this."

"No question," Lillian nodded.

"Thanks," Daniel said, and then let out a small laugh. "Man, I just don't understand why I'm afraid!"

"You don't have to understand it," said Lillian. "All you can do is accept it, and deal with it."

"Mom's right," Ken said. "It's OK to be afraid sometimes. Just don't let a little fear keep you from doing something extraordinary!"

"Thanks, Dad," said Daniel, feeling the strength that his parents had given him.

That evening they met up with Jake's family on the way to the airport. They arrived at Kennedy International Airport with plenty of time to spare, but all too soon the time came for them to go to their gate. They reached the security checkpoint, and it was time to say good-bye. They gave a quick good-bye to each other's family, and then moved on to their own. As Daniel was hugging his family good-bye, his sadness overcame him. He tried to tell them that he loved them and would miss them, but the lump in his throat prevented any words from escaping. And all the while he was fighting back the tears, holding them in at least until he walked away, so his family wouldn't have to see him cry. But try as he might, he could not stop the tears. Though he made no sound, the streams flowed freely down his cheeks. And then, in what he would always consider one of the hardest moments of his life, he turned and walked away, dragging his small carry-on suitcase behind him.

Once they had passed through security, Jake put his arm around Daniel's shoulders and said with a smile, "It's all right, you'll be fine."

Daniel straightened himself up just as Jeanne, his best friend from college, walked up.

"Hey!" she said with a big smile on her face. "So, I am, like, jumping out of my skin here. Aren't you?"

"Yeah, definitely," Daniel said. "Oh, by the way, Jeanne, this is my friend I told you about, Jake."

"Nice to meet you," Jeanne smiled.

Jeanne had dark hair and brown eyes, and was very pretty. She had on a backpack so large that it looked as though it came with a headrest. She was smiling wildly with excitement; in fact she very nearly seemed to be actually jumping out of her skin. She lived in Queens, only about a half hour away from where Daniel and Jake lived on Long Island. Like the boys, she was in her second year of college.

Although most people studied abroad when they were in their junior year, Jake would have been unable to because of his ROTC training. He was supposed to go back to school for training exercises in the beginning of the following August, and then not come back home again, even for breaks. So Daniel had decided to go abroad a year early, when Jake could go with him. When Jeanne had learned that Daniel was going his sophomore year, she decided to as well.

About halfway through the plane ride Jake turned to Jeanne and said, "Hey, want me to tell you a joke?"

Daniel laughed, warning, "Watch out, they're really bad."

But Jeanne agreed to hear the joke, and so Jake began. "OK, so two muffins are in the oven. One muffin turns to the other and goes, 'Man it's hot in here.' Then the other one looks back and says, 'Ahh! Talking muffin!'"

Jeanne stared at him dumbfounded as he began to laugh. His laugh was possibly the loudest and most obnoxious and contagious laugh in the history of the human race, and in the close quarters of the airplane it seemed even louder. Soon Daniel began to laugh, then Jeanne caught it, and the three of them laughed hysterically, waking nearly everyone on the plane.

When their laughter subsided, Daniel said, "I told you they were bad."

"Hey!" Jake replied. "My jokes are hysterical. You're laughing, aren't you?"

Daniel ignored Jake and kept talking to Jeanne. "You know, my dad actually banned Jake from telling jokes in his presence?" he said.

"Really? I didn't think it was *that* bad," Jeanne laughed.

"Oh, he's gotten better," Daniel said. "Tell the one that got you banned."

Jake cleared his throat, as if ready for a long speech. "OK," he said. "So an owl and a pigeon fly into a bar. One of them orders soup."

Jeanne waited for the ending, but that was it. Jake, of course, was hysterically laughing once again. "OK," said Jeanne. "Yeah, if you had told me that one, I would have banned you, too."

For the rest of the night they went back and forth telling jokes. When they ran out of jokes, they shared funny stories. By the time the plane landed, the three of them were old friends. In the terminal, they made their way to the center of the airport to figure out how to find the hotel where they would meet up with others from their program. There was no one there to meet them, and no bus. As they walked toward the exit to search for a taxi, Daniel pulled Jake aside.

"I can't do this," he whispered. "I can't do it alone."

"Look, you're never really alone," Jake said. "As long as you have people that love you and that you love, you're never really alone, even if you are by yourself. They are always with you, in your thoughts and in your heart."

Daniel paused for a second and smiled, looking at his best friend. "That was by far the most profound thing you've ever said."

"Well, I did have the entire eight-hour plane ride to think," Jake said with a smile. "So don't worry, it'll never happen again."

As the city was whipping past in the taxi, Daniel did his best to observe Paris. When he looked up, he saw that the city was gorgeous and unique. The tall buildings were remnants of a time long passed, testaments to the strength of ancient European architecture. And they were beautiful, each one ornate and unique. But when he looked down, it seemed that Paris was like any other modern city they had been to, full of modern stores and people. It truly was one of the most amazing cities in the world.

The next evening, they waited in the hotel lobby for their host families to arrive. Daniel's family showed up first. He had no idea of what to expect. When he approached, he saw a woman and a small boy. The woman looked as though she were in her mid to late sixties. Conversely, the boy appeared to be only five or six years old.

He smiled wide and said, *"Bonjour, je m'appelle Daniel."* *Hello, my name is Daniel.*

He gave the woman the gift he had brought, little trinkets from New York. Then the boy led Daniel to the car. When they got there Daniel became slightly worried; his suitcase was nearly as big as the car. With great effort he shoved the huge suitcase into the trunk of the clown car, and then climbed into the front seat.

Before he even had his seat belt buckled they were off, speeding through the city, weaving in and out of traffic. He quickly buckled up, and then his hand found the armrest on the door. For the rest of the ride, though his face showed no fear, his knuckles were white from strangling the handle.

Along the ride both the woman and the boy spoke quite a bit. Daniel had taken years of French, but was too tired to process much of what they said. He did, however, pick up the fact that there were six kids, and the older ones were already grownup, or at least teenagers. He also learned that he would be living slightly outside of Paris, in the *banlieu*, or suburbs. He was also told names and hobbies, none of which he really understood. The whole time he simply smiled politely, nodding his head in agreement and trying not to concentrate on how close they were coming to the cars next to them.

They arrived at the apartment, and quickly two teenage boys showed up to help Daniel with the bags. He was happy that he didn't have to carry his bags when he realized that they were on the fifth floor, and there were no elevators. He was shown his room, and then brought back downstairs where his hosts offered him a seat as they waited for dinner to be prepared. There he met his host father and the other two children. The father looked even older than the mother, possibly in his seventies. And, Daniel noted, all of the kids looked exactly like their father. Which was not fortunate for them.

Not long after they sat down at the table, the food was served. It looked like a strange mixture of snot and mushrooms. Daniel was still feeling somewhat queasy from the past two days of travel, so he only took a small portion. He finished everything that was given to him, though, knowing it was considered rude in France to do otherwise. Despite its strange appearance the food was actually rather tasty. He never did find out the true list of ingredients, and something told him he didn't want to know.

Even as Daniel was sitting down to the meal of snot (as it later came to be called), Jake was sitting and waiting for his "family." Finally, after literally hours, they showed up, greeted Jake, and brought him back to their small apartment. He said his goodnights, walked into his room and sat on his bed. It was extremely comfortable, much better than he had expected. As he unpacked he was pleasantly surprised to discover that there was more space in the room than he needed. But what surprised him most was when he was looking through the room and opened a cabinet to reveal a television. He turned it on and sat down on his bed, watching it and thinking about how the place exceeded all his expectations. Soon he fell into a deep, restful sleep such as he had not known in days.

Nearly two weeks after his brother had left for Paris, Gabe walked up to Robert, who was sitting at his locker before school started.

"Oversleep again?" Gabe asked, sitting down next to his best friend.

"How'd you know?" Robert asked back.

"You're wearing two different types of shoes," Gabe said, laughing. "But don't worry, it isn't really that noticeable."

"How do you wake up at 5:45 every day?" asked Robert.

"I set my alarm, and then I make sure that I don't sleep through it," Gabe responded.

"I don't sleep through it, I just hit the snooze," Robert retorted.

"Well, I don't do that either," said Gabe. "I don't understand. I mean, you are one of the most disciplined people I know, and yet you couldn't wake up if your life depended on it."

"Yeah, well let's just hope my life never depends on waking up to an alarm clock," Robert said as a beautiful girl walked by.

It was "Gorgeous Girl." Robert had been in love with her all year, even though he had never actually spoken to her. She had just moved to his school district this year. As soon as Gorgeous Girl had moved in, Robert had known he needed to get to know her. She was only a little over five feet tall, with long blonde hair and deep blue eyes. So far, however, Robert had not worked up the nerve to approach her, though he assured Gabe he was "getting there." Time seemed to freeze as she walked by, and Robert barely noticed the large boy walking up.

"Raines!" the boy yelled. "You were supposed to meet me after school yesterday so I could pound on you. But you never showed!"

"Yeah, I wonder why," Robert said sarcastically. "Why would I stay late and miss my bus home just so you could pound on me?"

"Umm …" said the boy, thinking hard. "Because I called you out! And now that you didn't show up everyone is gonna know you're a coward."

"Well, look," said Robert. "I don't really care if everyone thinks I'm a coward; that doesn't make it true. And I didn't stay because it would have been a waste of time. Why should I miss my bus just to show how weak you are?"

"You think you can beat me up?" asked the boy. "I'm twice your size!"

"Then why do you want to beat him up?" asked Gabe, interjecting. "So you can beat up a kid who's half your size? Yeah, that really shows that you're a tough guy."

Robert laughed, and the boy became enraged. He threw a punch at Gabe, who was leaning right on his locker. Gabe ducked out of the way, causing the boy to smash his knuckles into the metal locker. Gabe moved forward and put his foot right inside the boy's foot. Then he turned, causing the boy's leg to buckle. He fell forward, hitting his face into the locker. He wasn't really injured, just a little bumped, so he wouldn't swing at Gabe again. Gabe hated fighting, which was why he never threw a punch at the boy. All he did was defend himself.

A teacher who had been standing in the hall had seen the whole thing. He came over and commended Gabe and Robert for not getting into a serious fight, and for not having shown up the afternoon before. Then he informed the boy, who was just getting up, that he would be internally suspended for fighting and bullying. Gabe and Robert watched the teacher walk away with the boy in the direction of the dean's office.

"Sorry, didn't mean to get you involved there," Robert said.

"Oh, whatever, that guy had it coming," Gabe replied.

"Funny, though, most of the time people don't want to fight you," Robert said. "They only want to fight me."

"That's because you have a big mouth," Gabe answered with a smile.

"But whatever, that guy had no business wanting to fight you either way. He definitely got what he deserved."

It was then that the first bell rang. Being late was a serious offense, so they went their separate ways.

Shane was in school in plenty of time as well, and he just sat hanging out with his friends before class started. The beginning of his day went well, with nothing out of the ordinary happening. He even found out that he had aced a test that he had not been so sure of when he had taken it. In fact, he could honestly say that it was a good day, until lunch.

Shane and his friends had a nice lunchtime tradition. They would get in and eat their lunches as quickly as they could so they could go outside and play suicide. Suicide was a game played with a tennis ball against as big a wall as possible. The players would throw the ball against the wall, and then attempt to catch the ball as it came off. If a player dropped the ball he would have to run and touch the wall before another player could pick it up and throw it to the wall. If the ball hit before the player, that player received an out. After three outs the player would have to sit. Shane and his friends added in their own rules depending on the day, but this was how the game was generally played. It was a fun way to pass lunch. But if they did not eat quickly, they would lose the wall to the fifth graders. That day they were on their second game before any of the older kids even came outside.

There was one fifth grader whom Shane had always disliked, even though they had never officially met, and that was Melvin, the bully. The bully's dark hair wasn't parted or combed; it just kind of sat there in an unbridled mess. He also had the icky habit of wiping his constantly runny nose on his sleeve. But it wasn't his looks that Shane didn't like, it was his attitude. Melvin was the typical bully, bigger than any of the other kids, using his size to get what he wanted from the smaller kids. Shane had never had an encounter with the bully, but still he liked to steer clear of the kid.

As Shane and his friends were playing that day, Melvin and two of his brutish friends sauntered up.

"Our court, you losers off, now," said the bully.

Shane's friends said nothing, too petrified to speak. When he saw the state of his friends, Shane said, "We're already playing here; there's another court over there."

"Oh, look, the little hero. Well, *you* go use that court," said the bully. His brutish friends never said a word, they just pounded their huge fists into their palms.

"No, we won't. We were here first," said Shane. "Just because you're bigger doesn't give you the right to kick us off. We earned the right to be here, and we aren't leaving. If you keep this up, I'm going to tell a teacher."

"Do you want me to pound you?" Melvin cried in a rage.

"Sure, why not?" Shane said, shaking his head. "I haven't had a good pounding in weeks."

"All right, boys," said the bully. "Let's teach the little hero a lesson."

Shane's friends scattered as the three humongous boys advanced toward him. Shane backed up a little bit, and then planted his feet firmly and put his hands up. He hated to fight, but he did not seem to have any other choice here. The bully attacked with both hands over his head, possibly in an attempt to lie down on Shane and smother him. Shane was in no mood to play around, and quickly counterattacked by giving Melvin a light kick in the stomach. The bully doubled over for a second, holding his stomach and coughing. Then he lifted up his hands and attacked again. Shane let the bully come this time, and when Melvin came close enough, the smaller boy grabbed the outstretched hands and directed them toward the floor, turning his own body at the same time. Melvin sprawled onto his face. Shane looked at the two friends, who turned and ran away.

Shane leaned down to the bully and said, "Like I said, we were here first. I don't want to hurt you, so please, stay away from me and my friends from now on."

Shane walked away feeling pretty good about himself. He had defended himself without hurting anyone, but he also never had to worry about the bully bothering him again. His friends were jumping all over him calling him their hero. He walked back into the cafeteria feeling like the big man on campus. It was then that he was called, along with the bully, into the principal's office.

The principal of the school was a woman in her late forties, with straggly red hair and a mean scowl constantly hanging from her already wrinkled face. She had been good at inspiring fear in children while she was a teacher, and now that she was a principal she had perfected the art. Kids would get chills as they passed her office; legend had it that it was because she was staring at them through the wooden door. A common dare among students was to simply go up and touch the handle, and then run away as fast as possible. Shane shared the fear, but at the moment he was more perplexed than afraid. There was no reason that he should be in trouble.

As Shane walked in he noticed that it was in fact colder in the office, though he could see no air conditioner. He sat down in a chair in front of the desk, with the bully sitting next to him. He stared at the principal, wondering what she could possibly have to say, and how she could possibly have seen what had happened outside. But he was not worried; after all, the fight had not been his fault.

"What, exactly, happened?" asked the principal in a rough, icy voice.

Shane began to tell the story. "We were outside playing suicide …"

"Not you!" yelled the principal, interrupting. "Now, Melvin, darling, what happened?"

"Well, we were outside playing suicide when this kid came up," said the bully. "Then I told him we could share the court, but he refused. Then he started hitting me, and threw me on the ground."

"That's not true!" said Shane.

"Are you calling my son a liar?" asked the principal.

"Your son?" Shane asked in disbelief.

"Yes, my son," said the principal. "Are you calling him a liar?"

"Well, I'm not saying that he's lying, just that his side of the story might not be totally true," said Shane, getting worried.

"And what is your side?" asked the principal.

"Well, me and some of the other fourth graders were playing, and he came out and tried to steal our court," said Shane. "Then when I told him he couldn't have it, he attacked me. All I did was defend myself."

"So you are calling my son a liar!" yelled the principal.

"That's what happened!" said Shane. "Ask any of the other kids!"

"I don't have to ask anyone," said the principal. "I know my little angel would never do anything like that. So now you want to be a bully? I will not stand for bullies in my school. You think about that all week at internal suspension."

"That's not fair!" yelled Shane, a lump forming in his throat.

"Oh, so now you are yelling at me?" asked the Principal. "You want to be suspended next week, too?"

Shane stopped talking, and hung his head low. He looked at the bully, who sneered at him and stuck out his tongue. The principal came over, grabbed Shane by the back of the shirt, and dragged him out of her office. For a whole week, Shane would have to sit in the library all day long every day, including during lunch. He went home that day on the verge of tears. His mother was speaking to Daniel as he walked through the door.

Daniel hung up the phone a half hour later with mixed emotions. First he was proud of both of his brothers for standing up for themselves so well, and for doing it without really hurting anyone. Anyone could win a fight, but it takes a true warrior to win a fight without inflicting any damage. But also Daniel was extremely angry at the fact that a principal could be so blind as to what really happened. He was mostly upset with the injustice to his brother. And he was especially mad because, with him so far away, there was absolutely nothing he could do about it.

"You couldn't do anything about it even if you were there," said Jake after Daniel told him the story.

"I know, but still I could make him feel better, if nothing else," Daniel replied.

"You can do that from here," said Jake. "Anyway I don't think you should worry about it."

"Yeah, you know how I get though," said Daniel.

"I know, I know," said Jake. "You're just way too protective of your brothers. Other people are there who can help him."

"I know," Daniel responded. "But I wish I was there for him. It's stuff like this that makes me homesick."

"You're still homesick?" Jeanne asked.

"A little, but it's nothing I can't deal with," Daniel shrugged. "I think

I'll always be a little homesick, but I'm not giving up. Completing this is too important."

"You make it sound like a test," Jake said.

"It is," Daniel said. "In a way. I can give up any time I want. But not giving up will mean I'm stronger for the next test."

"I guess that makes sense," Jake said. "We all have our own tests to pass."

"Besides," Daniel said. "I couldn't have picked a cooler test."

"That's the truth," Jeanne said with a smile.

The first few months in Paris flew by. Each day they would sit in the same little park near Notre Dame and eat, and they noticed the weather getting better and better. Soon the trees had leaves, and the flowers were in bloom. Their park was blossoming, and other people were coming to share it with them. Then, on the weekends, they would come up with some fun place to visit, or some interesting area of Paris to walk through. They never suspected that the next few months would change their lives forever.

Chapter 2

Interesting Discovery

Jake and Daniel found that by late March they were really getting into the swing of things in Paris. They were speaking French fluently, or at least fluently enough to get them by. They had really learned their way around the city, too; they had visited every major monument in Paris, and even some of the less well-known ones. The weather was beautiful, so they spent most days relaxing outside in their park with the sun in their faces, thinking about how good life can be sometimes.

Friday, March 28, would be Jake's twentieth birthday. Both boys were both excited; first, because Jake's birthday usually fell while they were at school separately, and second, because it fell on a Friday. That meant they could go out and do whatever they wanted without having to worry about school the next day. They were going to go out to a club and spend the night having fun with their Paris friends.

They decided on a little club in the Latin Quarter that they had been to a few times before. It was a nice, cozy place that generally played music from the early 1980s United States collection. It didn't bother Jake or Daniel; they liked to dance to pretty much whatever music played. They had fun even though they were never the best dancers on the floor.

Jake invited Jeanne, but did not tell her that it was his birthday. He didn't want a big deal made, he just wanted to go out and have fun. Daniel got him a card that said, "Congratulations, you're a grandmother!" They never got each other serious cards, or even relevant ones for that matter. The last card that Jake had gotten Daniel had read, "Twelve is a tough age for a young lady, but I know you can do it!"

They met the others inside the club at around eleven o'clock that night. They surveyed the scene as they walked in. Everyone in the club seemed to be nicely dressed, and almost everyone was smiling. It was a refreshing scene against the stern faces and drab clothes they saw every day on the streets of Paris. Daniel and Jake were no exceptions; they were wearing their nicest khaki pants with black dress shoes. Jake was wearing a charcoal gray crewneck T-shirt, and Daniel was wearing a maroon, long sleeved V-neck shirt. Both were wearing their most charming smiles.

They decided to start the night just sitting around a table, taking in the atmosphere. Jake and Daniel sat facing the door, so that they could see everyone who came in. Jeanne sat next to Jake. They all sat around talking and laughing, sharing funny stories from childhood and their most recent escapades in Paris. Then, for maybe the first time since they had met, there was a lull in the conversation. Through the silence, they distinctly heard a strange and yet familiar formation of consonants and vowels into syllables and phrases.

"Wow, this place is pretty nice," said the strange voice.

"That's English!" Daniel exclaimed. It had been a while since they had heard English spoken by people other than themselves. It stuck out in the crowd, and intrigued them. The owner of the voice sat down with a friend at a table behind them. They began to have a low conversation. Daniel leaned back in his chair to hear them, but they were still talking too low. So he leaned farther, and farther, and then ... too far! The chair tipped and he went crashing to the floor. He quickly sprang up as though nothing had happened, and began brushing himself off. Jake's laughter overpowered the loud music of the club.

The owner of the voice looked at him with surprise. He looked at the owner and his jaw dropped. It was a girl, about his age, and possibly the most beautiful girl he'd ever laid eyes on. She was maybe four or five inches shorter than Daniel, and her body was slender and athletic.

She had long, straight black hair with sparkling blue eyes, and rosy pink cheeks that were lightly dusted with freckles. She had absolutely the most incredibly dazzling smile ever. Her friend was shorter, with blonde hair and a slightly thicker build, but also very pretty.

"Good looking, but obviously not very bright," said the first girl to her friend. Then, she turned to Daniel and said, "*Bonjour, je m'appelle Jamie.*" *Hello, my name is Jamie.*

Daniel finished brushing himself off, then extended his hand with a smile, saying, "Nice to meet you Jamie, my name is Daniel."

Jamie's face went bright red. "I'm sorry; I didn't know you spoke English! I, uh …"

"No, don't worry," said Daniel, still smiling. "That wasn't graceful, it's true. And, frankly, I'm flattered that the most beautiful girl I've ever seen thinks I'm good looking!" He sat down and began talking to the two girls.

Jake, seeing his friend's … grave situation, felt obliged to … ease some of the pressure now on Daniel. "Hi, I'm Jake."

Jamie and Daniel were already engrossed in a conversation of their own, so Jamie's friend looked up, smiled at Jake, and said, "Hi, I'm Liz." He was absolutely dazzled.

He sat down next to her, and they began having a very nice conversation, which eventually became entwined with Daniel and Jamie's. As it turned out, the two girls were also from Long Island, only a little further east in a town called Islip. They were the same age as Daniel and Jake, also spending the last half of their sophomore year abroad, though with a different program. They had been best friends since they met in middle school and thought of each other as sisters more than friends. Jake and Daniel found the girls to be very charming and intelligent, the latter of which was a very important characteristic for them to find in a girl. The conversation was natural and relaxed, and they found themselves smiling the whole time.

Jake was his usual self. "Wanna hear a joke?" he asked.

"Yeah, definitely!" answered Liz. Jamie nodded in agreement.

Jake stood up and put his hands in front of him: It was his preferred joke telling position. "OK, so these three guys bust out of jail, but they're being followed by the police, so they hide out in a barn. The police come in, and shine a flashlight on the cows. The guy hiding behind the cows goes, 'MOO!!!!' so the policemen think it's just a bunch of cows. Then they shine the light on a bunch of horses, and the guy behind the horses goes, 'NEIGH!!!!' so the policemen think it's just a bunch of horses. Then they shine the light on a sack of potatoes, so the guy behind the potatoes goes, 'POTATO!!!!'"

Daniel always laughed at Jake's jokes, and of course so did Jake, so the two of them started rolling with laughter in the middle of the French club, Jake's laugh once again overpowering the blasting music. To their surprise, Jamie and Liz were laughing hysterically, too. Whether it was at the joke, or at Jake's infectious laugh, they were definitely unable to control their own hysterics. The four of them sat around the small table in the corner of the club just laughing, trying to keep their stomachs from hurting too much while they kept rolling away.

When they finally stopped laughing, Jamie grabbed Daniel's hand, pulled him up and said, "Let's go dance."

Daniel didn't have a chance to argue, nor did he want to. He loved to dance. As he and Jamie were getting up, Liz dragged Jake up, though he barely put up a struggle. They had been dancing for a few minutes when Daniel saw Jeanne. He realized that he and Jake had totally forgotten about her. Jeanne signaled for Daniel and Jake to come over. When they did, she informed them that she was leaving. Jake and Daniel apologized, said their good-byes, and then headed back to the dance floor to meet up with Jamie and Liz. But when they got closer, they saw the two girls dancing with two new guys. Their hearts sank, and they were beginning to walk away when they noticed something unsettling.

Jamie and Liz seemed to be turning away from the other guys, trying to walk away to find a new spot to dance. But every time they did, the other guys would step in front and stop them. Finally one of the guys, both of whom were far larger than either Jake or Daniel, grabbed Jamie's arm, very hard. She pulled away, pushed him away, and went to move.

Daniel saw the guy's hand come up, and his heart jumped. He was going to hit Jamie! He and Jake ran forward to stop it, but they were too far away; the hand went flying toward Jamie's face. As the hand was about to land, however, Jamie blocked. She quickly grabbed the wrist with her right hand while pushing just above the elbow with her left. The result was a very powerful and very painful arm bar. She then leaned her weight on the man's back. The pressure sent a shockwave of pain through his body, which pushed the man onto his stomach, his arm still off to the side, pinned to the ground by Jamie's knee.

As soon as Jamie had pinned the one man, his friend moved in to attack. Liz grabbed his arm to stop him. He turned and broke free, then tried to push her away with his right hand. She met it with her right hand, palm to palm. She then rotated her hand, grabbing his pointer finger. Using only a small amount of pressure she bent the finger, which sent crippling pain rushing through him. She completely controlled him, bringing him down onto his face with his arm in front of him, putting just enough pressure to keep him there. The bouncers came, took the two men from Liz and Jamie, and threw them out of the club. Everyone surrounding the dance floor was thoroughly impressed, but Daniel and Jake were in love.

It was already about 4:00 a.m. by that point, so the new foursome decided to leave the club. The girls were getting tired, anyway. The Métro would open in a little over an hour, so they decided to walk and talk until that time. Daniel and Jake found out that the girls were second degree black belts in Ninjitsu, a martial art very similar to their own. They also talked about things that they all knew from Long Island and just about their lives in general. For the next two hours they walked and talked, and by the time six o'clock rolled around they knew almost everything there was to know about each other. At six they found themselves near the Odéon Métro stop on the line four, which was Jamie and Liz's line, so they decided to go. Daniel and Jake said good-bye, and then walked in the direction of the Châtelet Métro stop on the line one, which would take them to Daniel's apartment.

Paris being so far north, the sun was not yet up at six o'clock in the morning when they walked past the Notre Dame cathedral. It was marvelously lit at night, shining brightly over all the lights in the area. Daniel and Jake decided they were not ready to go home yet, so they went to their little park to sit and talk for a while.

"Good birthday?" Daniel asked.

"*Great* birthday," Jake answered. "And, man, those girls are awesome."

"Yeah, no kidding," Daniel said. "We'll be seeing them again real soon, I hope."

"Same here," said Jake, taking in the beauty of Notre Dame.

"Isn't it funny, though?" asked Daniel after a second.

"What?"

"Well, I mean what are the odds?" Daniel continued. "What are the odds that we would go all the way to Paris just to meet two incredible girls from Long Island?"

"That is strange," said Jake. "But I guess that's just the way fate works."

"And they're amazing girls, too!" said Daniel, obviously very excited. "I mean they're martial artists, and good ones, as we've seen. They're a lot of fun to be around, and we seem to have a lot in common with them."

"Not to mention they're beautiful," Jake added.

"Yes, they are," Daniel added with a small sigh.

They both sat thinking about all that had happened that night. All of a sudden, a violent scream pierced the peaceful night. Jake and Daniel both shot up, looking around but saying nothing for fear of missing another scream. Sure enough, another scream followed shortly after the first one, the second one equally as bloodcurdling as the first. Without a word to each other, the boys took off in the direction of the screams.

They ran as fast as they could toward the repeated screams, not paying attention to what turns they made along the way. Any thoughts of fatigue faded, even though it was six o'clock in the morning and they had been out all night. All they could think about was that they might be too late, that they might not be fast enough to help. Soon they found themselves running into a small alley where they found the source of the screams.

They saw a frightened woman, clutching the hand of a small boy. The boy, clad in a school uniform, was holding what appeared to be a small backpack. They were cornered by six men, shouting wildly and waving weapons around. One of the men was rifling through the woman's purse, while another was pushing his knife against her throat, talking to her in a low, intimidating grumble.

"*Avez vous besoin d'aide?*" Daniel asked her as he ran up. *Do you need help?*

She nodded frantically, though it was no longer up to her if the young strangers got involved. The man closest to her turned as Daniel ran up, throwing a punch at the black belt's face. Daniel was too fast, however, and ducked out of the way of the punch, delivering a devastating shot to the man's ribs as he moved. Then he swept out the man's feet, sending him to the ground. He finished with a hard punch that left the attacker unconscious. A man holding a club attacked, but Jake got in his way. He ran at Jake and swung straight for his face. Jake stepped in and used the attacker's weight against him, throwing the attacker over his hip onto the pavement. The wind rushed out of the man's lungs so fast that he passed out.

Seeing his two companions on the ground, the man holding the boy released his hostage and lunged out with the knife, aiming for Daniel's chest. Daniel defended himself with the same move he had used on Gabe at his last night of Ju-Jitsu. The man quickly found himself on his back, relieved of the knife. Because the man had attacked him with a knife, Daniel had not held back, and now the man was rolling in agony. His arm was broken. Another man attacked Jake at the same time that Daniel was attacked, wrapping his arms tightly over Jake's around the younger man's chest. Jake once again used his opponent's weight against him, doing a similar throw to the one he had just done.

The last two were both unarmed. One walked up to Daniel, somewhat warily. He seemed to hold himself as though he had some martial arts knowledge. Daniel guessed from the stance that it was Tae Kwon Do, and so he figured that the man would try to kick at him, most likely in the face. He was right: The fighter threw his right leg out at Daniel's face. It was a fast and deadly kick, but Daniel was ready for it. He dropped to the ground, spinning around on his left knee. His right foot swept around and took out the man's leg, sending him flat on his back. Daniel finished with a powerful punch to the face, and the man was out.

While Daniel was facing off against his foe, Jake had a challenge of his own. The last attacker was eyeing him, searching for a weakness. Jake stood without moving, glaring at his nervous opponent. Jake saw the kick fly at Daniel's face, and turned to see what happened. His opponent saw this and ran forward, just like Jake had wanted. The young American blocked the punch, and as he did he threw his body up into the air, almost parallel to the ground. He wrapped one hand around the man's neck and turned. This flipped the man over Jake's body, onto his back, with Jake coming down on top of him. The force of the throw, combined with Jake's body weight landing directly on top of him, left the man unconscious.

The beauty of Ju-Jitsu was that it could be done in two different ways. It could be done softly, using the techniques to control an opponent and avoid danger. Or it could be done hard, the force of the moves breaking bones, dislocating joints, and sometimes rendering an attacker unconscious. Either style was completely effective in self-defense; it was up to the user to decide which style the situation called for. Had they been attacked in a schoolyard, they might have used the soft style until someone could break up the fight. But having been attacked in a dark alley at night by people with weapons, they had no choice but to use the hard style. Their attackers wouldn't be getting up for a while.

While there was no more danger from the attackers, they were still standing in a dark alley in the wee hours of the morning, so they didn't want to stick around. Before they left, however, they walked up to the woman and her son.

"*Merci, merci beaucoup!*" said the woman. *Thank you! Thank you so much!*

She smiled and ran off with her son. Daniel and Jake walked toward the entrance of the alley.

"I hate fighting," said Daniel as they walked.

"Me, too, so senseless," Jake replied. "But we had no choice. They didn't seem to wanna talk."

Daniel did not answer. They had reached the end of the alley. He was looking around and so was Jake, realizing that they did not remember how they got there. They were lost, at 6:15 a.m. on the streets of Paris. The sun still had not risen, and probably would not for another hour. They looked around in silence until they saw a silver light shining nearby.

It was a strange light, obviously not natural, and like no streetlight they had ever seen. But for some strange reason it called to them, beckoning them to follow it. Almost as if on their own, their feet brought them toward the light. As they moved closer, however, it moved away. It moved into another alley, and they followed it, completely mystified by its power. At the end of the alley was a tunnel, and the light went inside, so they did, too.

As soon as they stepped inside the tunnel, the spell was broken. They shook their heads, and then turned to walk out. But when they turned around, the entrance was gone. They realized that they had no choice but to continue, to follow the strange light wherever it took them. They started on, unable to see anything but the light, which always kept just out of reach.

It wasn't long before they realized that the tunnel was descending. If it hadn't been for the decline, they would never have known that they were moving at all, because the light always stayed the same distance from them. They couldn't tell how far underground they were, nor could they tell if they were any closer to their destination. All they knew was that the air was slowly getting thicker, and hotter.

Soon the sweat began pouring out from their bodies, and their breath became slow and labored. The pressure was also building, making it difficult for them to even walk. Their hands reached out on their own to feel for the walls for any support. Their feet moved only out of habit; Daniel and Jake had almost completely lost control of themselves.

Daniel was the first one to hit the floor, and Jake soon followed. The pressure had taken its toll, and the heat continued to assault them from all sides. They could not move. They could not even force themselves to crawl.

Daniel managed to form words. "Jake, I can't get up."

"Me, neither," said Jake. "I can't even move."

"Why did we follow that darn light?" asked Daniel.

"I don't know," Jake answered. "It was hypnotic; I couldn't control myself."

Daniel looked up to scowl at the light, always hovering just out of reach. But as he looked at it he noticed something. The light was now stationary, not moving anymore. More importantly, however, it was actually coming out of a room.

"Jake, the light!" Daniel shouted.

Jake looked up and saw what Daniel was talking about. "So we're almost there," he said.

"Yeah!" Daniel responded. "We can make it, all we have to do is move a little further."

"Then let's do it!"

They struggled slowly to their feet, pushing against the air, their fatigue, and their own muscles just to get up. Once they were upright again they stumbled on, calling on whatever strength they had in reserve. Neither of them thought about what could be at the destination, they only thought about reaching it. Somehow they knew that as long as they made it that far, they would be fine. Finally, on the last brink of consciousness, they crossed the threshold into the room with the silver light.

As soon as they made it into the room, they felt their energy return. The tremendous pressure was gone, as was the oppressive heat. And their muscles were completely rejuvenated. They barely noticed this, however, as they were much more interested in this strange room and the strange silver light. They looked to one side of the room and saw something that caught their attention. It was a pedestal about knee height, upon which rested a shield. Laid across the shield was a medieval-style sword.

They ran up and looked at it. It was covered in dust, as though it had been there for a thousand years. Fixed onto the sword's hilt was a strange gem. The gem was dark blue, almost purple, and it looked almost sad. It did not sparkle at all in the light. Fascinated, Daniel reached out and grabbed the hilt. He wrapped his hand around the handle and pulled, but the sword didn't budge. He pulled with all of his might, but the sword would not move.

Jake stepped up behind him. "Let me try," he said.

Daniel stepped out of the way as Jake walked up. When he drew near, the sword seemed to come alive. It rose up until only the very tip was touching the shield. The hilt was now about chest height for Jake, and the sword spun around so the dark blue gem faced away from him.

Now facing him was a brilliant sapphire gem that glowed almost as brightly as the room itself. The dust that had covered the sword seconds earlier was gone. Jake grabbed the sword by the handle, and a sapphire blue light exploded out of him.

It was blindingly bright, causing Daniel, the stupefied onlooker, to stumble back. He fell into something as he did, and then hit the ground. The light from Jake was so blinding that Daniel was forced to look away and saw what he had stumbled over: another sword! It was similar to the first one, though it had an olive green gem on it. This gem also looked sad, and even with the added light in the room, it reflected none. As Daniel observed the sword, the blue light subsided, so he looked back at Jake.

What he saw made his jaw drop. It was Jake without a doubt, but he was completely different. First of all, his clothes had completely changed. He was now wearing a black suit of some sort, which covered his whole body, his hands and feet, and part of his neck. His face was unprotected except for a small mask across the eyes.

On the suit were various marks, all of that same sapphire blue, almost like gems themselves. There was one on the middle of his chest, one covering each of his shoulders, then along his forearms and thighs. Along with different clothes, Jake's attitude had changed. He was stone serious, and did not say a word. Daniel looked at him expectantly, but all Jake did was motion to the green sword.

Daniel turned around and saw that the green sword was rising up just as the blue sword had. It spun around to reveal a brilliant emerald gem opposite the olive colored one. Daniel reached out and grabbed the sword. The emerald light exploded from him, and he looked down to see what was happening to him. Within the light he saw a wave shoot across his body, starting at the right hand and continuing over the rest of his body. As the wave passed, Daniel's clothes were transformed into the same type of suit as Jake's, green where his was blue. When the wave had fully passed, the light faded, and Daniel was left standing there holding the sword.

They stood in silence for a moment, staring at each other speechlessly in the silver light. Then, Daniel spoke.

"Well, this is … interesting," he said.

"Yeah," Jake replied. "It feels like my body is about to explode."

"Mine, too," said Daniel. "This power is incredible; it's like nothing I have ever felt before. I feel like I could lift a bus."

"I know, same here," said Jake. "And the outfits are pretty cool, not to mention the swords."

"I know, but how did they get here?" Daniel asked.

Jake was about to answer when a mysterious voice said, "I put them here."

The voice came from all around them, from the walls and the ceiling. They looked around, but saw no one.

"And who are you?" Jake asked the mysterious voice.

The silver light in the room rushed together into one point. It formed into the shape of a man. He had a medieval-style cloak covering his silver body, with a trimmed goatee surrounding his mouth and a bald head. The shining silver figure spoke to them in a deep, booming voice. "I am Mercury, the guardian of the swords."

"Guardian?" Daniel asked in wonderment.

"Yes, it is my job to keep the swords safe, and out of the wrong hands," said Mercury. "I have waited here for nearly a thousand years, waiting for the day when the inheritors would step forward and claim their weapons."

"How do you know that we are not the wrong hands?" Jake asked.

"You were chosen for a specific purpose," Mercury replied. "What that purpose is, I cannot now say, but you would not have been chosen if you did not have that purpose."

"Well, that certainly clears things up," Daniel said, sarcastically.

"Do not worry, Daniel, everything will be made clear in time," said Mercury.

"You know my name?" Daniel asked.

"Of course, I know everything about you," Mercury said. "It is a gift that I have."

"Well, who are you?" Jake asked.

"I am Mercury, the guardian of the swords, Jacob."

"Well, yeah, I got that," Jake replied. "But who were you before you were guardian of the swords?"

"I was a sorcerer," said Mercury. "I created the swords, and so my fate is intertwined with them."

"So, are you … ?" Jake asked.

"Yes, I am a ghost," said Mercury. "But we will discuss this all at another time. For now, simply concentrate on your new powers, and your new duties."

"New duties?" Daniel asked.

"Yes, you are now more powerful than any other human on this planet," said Mercury. "But surely power is no good unless it is put to use. So how will you use this new power you have found?"

"We can do anything we want with it?" Daniel asked.

"Yes, and it can undoubtedly bring you anything you desire," said Mercury. "So what will you choose to bring yourselves?"

"Well, I think I speak for Jake as well when I say that we'd like to use our powers to help others," said Daniel. "I mean, power really exists to protect those who have none."

"I agree," said Jake. "If our new powers are as incredible as I think, then we could do a lot of good."

"Excellent, I had a feeling you would say that," said Mercury. "Then we can get to work tomorrow."

"Get to work?" Jake asked.

"Well, yes, training you to use this marvelous new power of yours," Mercury replied. Then he noticed that Daniel had a troubled look on his face. "What is wrong, Daniel?"

"Well, no offense, but these disguises are not very good," Daniel answered. "I mean, with just a small mask across his eyes, I can still tell it's Jake."

"I was just coming to that," said Mercury. "The armor, you will find, is tight and thick, but does not restrict your movements at all. And the masks are not for disguise."

"So no secret identities, then?" asked Daniel, disappointed.

"For people who do not know you, you do not need a disguise. And for those who do know you, no disguise would keep them from recognizing who you are," said Mercury. "You should not keep things from them anyway; they may wind up helping you in your endeavors. The masks are more to protect your eyes."

"Protect our eyes?" Jake asked.

"From what?" asked Daniel.

"Well, your transportation is quite intense," said Mercury. "And when you are moving at over two hundred miles per hour, your eyes will undoubtedly need some protection."

"*What???*" Jake and Daniel shouted at the same time.

"Ah, yes, here is your transportation. I am afraid that their previous owners did not appreciate their full value. But I am sure that they will better suit you two," Mercury said, lifting up his right hand.

As he did, the two shields came alive. They lifted off of their resting places, and Daniel and Jake watched as they began to spin around rapidly, doing barrel rolls in the air. Their colors brightened as they did, and soon they were completely emerald and sapphire. When the colors had fully appeared, they stopped spinning and just hovered a foot above the ground.

"There you are," said Mercury. "They are magnetized, so they will hold your swords when you do not need them. Also, the bottoms of your boots contain trace amounts of a special metal so that you do not fall off while flying. The metal in the boots will not attach to anything besides your shields, so you will not need to worry about accidentally sticking to something that you do not wish to stick to."

"OK, but then how do we get off?" Jake asked.

"Well, you control them mentally," replied Mercury. "You control their speed, their direction, whether or not they are magnetized, and what they attract when they are magnetized."

"Cool," said Daniel. "So if we don't wanna hold the swords all the time we just put them on the shields?"

"No," said Mercury. "If the swords come out of contact with either you or your armor, you become normal again. While you are in this state but not using your swords, you can put them in their scabbards."

"But there are no scabbards," said Jake.

"When they are not in use they disappear, so as not to get in your way," said Mercury. "Touch the blade flat on your back."

They did as Mercury said, and as they did, they felt their armor start to stir. Then, in response to their will, it jumped out, surrounding the blades to form scabbards. The boys slowly lowered their hands, and found that the swords stayed in their places in the newly formed scabbards. Just to check, they pulled swords out, and as they did, the scabbards rejoined their armor. Then, they re-sheathed the swords.

"OK, before you get to use your new toys, let me explain something," Mercury said. "You have around two months left here, which will be your time to train. You should be ready to fight by the time you get back to the States."

"Where are we going to train?" asked Jake. "It's a little cramped in here."

"There is a large wooded area near where Daniel lives called the Bois de Boulogne. It is an open space, so you have room, but it is secluded, so we will not be interrupted," replied Mercury. "Meet me at the Bois at 9:00 p.m. tomorrow. For now, enjoy your new gifts. The door to the tunnel is now open, but it will close for all time in exactly one minute."

They wasted no time; they hopped on their shields and shot off up the tunnel, careful not to run into the walls, but with enough speed to escape the tunnel in time. They found that the atmosphere was not oppressive with their new strength. They swept out of the tunnel just as it closed, for the last time. They swept out along the Seine River, and decided to really see what they could do.

They pushed their shields to full speed along the Seine. They varied their altitude, at some points flying high above the bridges, at others actually touching the waters, sending huge waves out onto the banks. They jumped over the bridges, releasing themselves from the shields and then catching them on the other side.

They were having the time of their lives. They would rise high in the air so that they could barely see the city. Once they were up as high as they could bear, they would release themselves and freefall, having the shields rescue them just feet from the ground. They reached the Eiffel

Tower, and decided to watch the sunrise from its top. It was truly a marvelous sight. Then they jumped away, spanning a great distance.

They spent about an hour and a half with their new gifts. It was eight in the morning: They had been out all night. They decided to get as much sleep as they could before they had to get up. They were on their way to Daniel's house, but decided that they would not take the Métro. They had other means of transportation in mind. They made it from the Eiffel Tower to the Les Sablons Métro stop in less than five minutes, beating the Métro by about twenty. As they ran toward Daniel's apartment they found his host father on his way to work. They asked for permission for Jake to stay there, and then ran upstairs.

"Not a bad day, all in all," said Jake.

"Not bad at all," said Daniel, as he fell asleep.

Chapter 3

Making the Most

The next night, after a very nice dinner with Jamie and Liz, Daniel and Jake hurried to a small clearing in the middle of the Bois de Boulogne. It was there that they met Mercury for their first day of training.

"Welcome, gentlemen," Mercury said as they approached. His silver shimmer and the moonlight were the only light in the clearing. "You two are late."

"Sorry, we got hung up," said Daniel as they ran up.

"Yes, the ladies are very lovely, I would have gotten 'hung up' as well," Mercury said with a smile.

"How did you … ?" Jake asked incredulously.

"I know much that you do not yet know about," Mercury replied. "But enough about that. Let us begin. What do you know of swordplay?"

"Only that it's not play at all," Jake said sarcastically. "If you're not careful, someone could put out an eye."

"Very nice," Mercury said, waiting for Daniel to control his laughter. "I'll take that to mean that you know little to nothing."

"Well, why do we need to know how to sword fight?" Daniel asked.

"If you have a sword, you should know how to use it," Mercury replied. "Anyone can swing a sword around and eventually hit a target, but finesse is a different issue. There will be times, you may find, that being able to manipulate your sword will give you a sharp edge over an opponent."

"Oh, I get it." Daniel laughed.

"Get what?" asked Jake.

"'Sharp edge,' 'sword,'" Daniel said. "Get it?"

"You're an idiot," Jake said, shaking his head.

"Hey, don't be bitter just because I got it first," Daniel said, still laughing.

"Stop, just stop," said Jake. "Before he takes the swords away because you're an idiot."

"He wouldn't do that," Daniel said.

"WILL YOU TWO FOCUS?" Mercury boomed. Once the two friends settled into silence, he added, "Thank you. In any case, you need to learn how to use your swords. Otherwise, they are simply decorations, which can become extremely dangerous both to you and those around you. So you will learn swordplay. Beyond that you will learn to improve your skills when you are not in contact with the swords. The more powerful you are on your own, the more powerful you will be with the swords."

"Sounds good," Daniel said. "Let's get to it."

"I was not finished," Mercury said sharply. "You will spend a half hour per day on conditioning and honing your skills. However, you must also learn to control your power while in contact with the swords. Power that cannot be controlled is useless. You will spend an hour each day learning control, which includes riding your shields. Then you will spend a final half hour each day meditating. This will hone your mind, and make it aware of things you never were aware of before. Understand?"

"Yes," Jake and Daniel replied at the same time.

"Two hours is a long time to train every day," said Jake.

"Are you saying that you cannot handle the rigorous training?" Mercury asked.

"I don't think that's what he's saying at all," said Daniel. "It's just a lot of time each day. But it's OK, we love training."

"Exactly!" said Jake.

"Excellent, let's get started then." Mercury said. "Let's begin by learning the art of the sword, which you might call 'fencing.'"

Mercury pointed to a small tree stump, on which rested two practice sabers and two masks. Daniel and Jake walked over to the stump, grabbed the swords, and their training began. The first day they learned basic fencing positions and basic movements of the sword. Then they showed Mercury exactly what they could do in terms of their Ju-Jitsu, their acrobatic skills, their strength and speed. Mercury was very impressed with all of these, especially the Ju-Jitsu skills that they had honed over years of training.

"Why do we have to learn to control our power again?" Daniel asked at the beginning of the second part of their training for the night.

"Because power with no control is useless, and dangerous," Mercury replied.

"But we know how to control our power," Jake protested.

"Is that so?" Mercury asked. "In that case, punch a crack that goes exactly halfway into that boulder over there."

Jake walked over to the boulder. Jake thought nothing of the fact that there was a random boulder in the middle of a grassy clearing. The boulder was large and thick, and would take a devastating punch just to crack it at all, let alone halfway. Even though Jake had the sword in its sheath across his back and the added power it gave him, he did not think it would be enough. Jake hauled off and swung his fist at the boulder. As he hit, the giant rock shattered into thousands of tiny pieces. Jake looked at his gloved fist in disbelief.

"Try again," Mercury said.

Mercury held up his hand, and the boulder reconstructed itself. This time Jake held back, barely tapping the boulder. Nothing happened, not even a tiny chip. Jake swung again, with only slightly more force. The boulder shattered once again into thousands of tiny pieces. Mercury reconstructed the stone, and Daniel tried his luck. No matter how many times either of them tried, the boulder either did not crack, or shattered completely.

"Now imagine that was a person," Mercury said. "You either just killed him, or did no damage."

"Very well then, control it is," said Jake.

"Agreed," said Daniel, still marveling at his ability to destroy the giant boulder, both amazed and afraid of his new power.

The training was intense. Mercury pushed them to their physical and mental limits, and then demanded more. Daniel felt his strength leaving him, felt his body start to break. His knees buckled, and his eyes closed on their own. Instantly, the image of Gabe and Shane flashed before him. His eyes shot open, and he felt his strength return. He pushed himself even harder than before. Then, the next time he felt his body begin to fail, he closed his eyes again. This time it was the image of his parents. The next time it was his friends. Then Jamie. Each time he felt himself start to break, the image of one of his loved ones would blaze in front of him. The people he loved gave him the strength to continue.

By the time the third part of the training, meditation, came around, he was more than ready for a break. During meditation they simply focused on their breathing, allowing all thoughts to leave their heads. They could hear the wind rustling through the trees, feel it cooling them as it whipped the sweat from their faces. They could hear the stream trickling along, following its path yet always slowly forming a new one. They could smell the grass and the trees.

At one point during meditation Daniel's contact lenses were bothering him, so he opened his eyes to fix them. He was surprised to find that Mercury had disappeared. He thought nothing of it, however, and quickly went back to his meditation. It seemed to them that all too soon their half hour was up, and it was time to go home. Mercury had returned, and relayed to them how pleased he was with their first day. He waved good-bye and then, with the swords, disappeared. Daniel walked Jake to the Métro, and then went back to his apartment. Their first day of training had gone very well, and they went home tired and happy.

As the days went on, the boys learned more and more. Their skills with the swords were improving rapidly, as were their abilities with the shields. In less than two weeks, they were able to push the shields to their top speeds, and close to their top altitudes. They were also getting used to their armor. Jake, never having worn glasses, still needed to get used to the mask. Daniel needed to get used to the tightness of the armor, being somewhat claustrophobic about tight clothing.

One day, around two weeks after their first day of training, Jake and Daniel decided to take a walk instead of heading straight back home after training.

"Imagine if I hadn't talked you into coming to Paris?" Daniel asked.

"Imagine if I hadn't talked you into staying?" Jake responded.

"Good point," Daniel laughed. "This really has been an interesting semester. I mean we're learning to speak French and staying with families that are completely unlike our own."

"Yeah, it's been fun," Jake said. "Not to mention the fact that we met some amazing girls, and found thousand-year-old swords that give us incredible power, badass armor, and flying shields."

"Oh, yeah, that too," Daniel said with a smile. "Which kinda makes me wonder. I mean, what if we had never come to Paris, or what if we had never gone out for your birthday? Or what if we had never met the girls, because we would have left with Jeanne and the others? Or when we heard the scream, what if we hadn't helped that lady?"

"You're gonna make your brain hurt," Jake answered. "You always overanalyze. Just let it go, we found the swords either by luck or by design, it doesn't matter. All that matters is what we do with what we were given."

"True," said Daniel. "Yeah, I guess you're right. It's strange to think how things work out sometimes. But no matter what, we're going to be the greatest heroes of all time, right?"

"You better believe it!" Jake answered, shaking his friend's hand. "Wait 'til we tell Gabe, Robbie, and Shane. They're gonna be so jealous!"

"Ha, yeah, it's a shame they can't have swords, too," Daniel said.

They did not see it, but there was a silver shimmer of light as Mercury disappeared. Jake and Daniel kept walking, never suspecting that they were being watched. And so they continued their adventures, spending as much time with Jamie and Liz as possible. Jeanne joined them more often than not, and they were developing into a nice group. Daniel and Jake trained with Mercury every night. And so their time in Paris passed, with every single day bringing its own adventure.

Gabe, Robert, and Shane had no idea of the adventures their brothers were having in Europe. Gabe had detected a little bit of excitement in Daniel's voice the last few times they spoke, but he knew Daniel had met a new girl, one that he really liked, so Gabe figured that was it. Jake was a little better at hiding his feelings to Robert, so Robert knew very little about what was happening. He knew a little bit about some girl named Liz that his brother was seeing. And Shane knew only that Daniel was having fun in Paris without him.

Truth be told, Shane was not having a very good time back on Long Island. Fourth grade was not all he had expected it to be, especially with the principal on his back. Her son had been bullying him constantly, and Shane was not one to take abuse without defending himself. But every time he defended himself, even though nobody got hurt, the principal would give him one full week of in school suspension. And the bully, her wonderful darling son who could never do anything wrong, always got off with nothing. Just once he'd like for someone to see what happened, and to hear her admit that he was right. But he knew that would never happen, so he struggled on, day by day.

Robert still couldn't work up the courage to talk to the gorgeous girl. He knew very little about her. He knew that she had just moved in from another town, and that she only had a few friends in the district. She had one friend, her best friend to be exact, and that friend was someone that Robert knew, or at least was acquainted with. The friend, Lauren, was generally in some of Gabe's classes each year. Lauren, Robert had heard, had a serious crush on his best friend. So it would work out perfectly, if he could only convince Gabe to ask Lauren out.

See, Gabe knew that Lauren liked him, as did a few other girls that he knew of. And it was not that they were bad people, or hideously ugly or anything. Actually, he quite liked them and found them to be very pretty. And he knew that if he just asked they would say yes and he would have a date. But that was secretly what he was afraid of. He was never afraid of rejection; that, he knew he could handle. He was actually afraid of them saying yes, of having to go out on a date. He just wouldn't know what to do, what to say. So he made up his mind that he would not ask a girl out until he had a chance to talk to the only person he had always been able to talk to.

That person was still in Paris, getting ready to begin his journey home. Daniel said a heartfelt good-bye to his host family and headed to the airport. He was taking the plane with Jake and Jeanne. Jamie and Liz had gone home a few days earlier, and were eagerly awaiting the return of the three friends they had made while in Paris. The plane ride was fairly uneventful. They sat and talked about the last five months, the fun they had had, and the personal struggles they had overcome. Jake and Jeanne joked with Daniel about his behavior in the airport on their first day in France, so long before.

By the time the aircraft had come to a full and complete stop, and the captain turned off the "fasten seat belts" sign, Daniel felt as though he was going to explode from the excitement. He stood up, mentally cursing the slow people in front of them. He was beginning to wish that Mercury had let them fly home on the shields, even though he said that they would not be able to go such a long distance. Finally, they were off the plane, and then they got to wait on the customs line. After the six-hour plane ride, what was an extra hour waiting to be let into their country of origin? As he walked through the customs line and into the waiting area, a broad, involuntary smile spread across his face. He was about to see the most important people in his life!

Their families were in the waiting area, patiently awaiting their triumphant return. As the travelers burst through the doors, Shane ran up and knocked Daniel over, baggage and all, with a gigantic hug. As Jake helped Daniel up, the others welcomed them back. It was a joyful reunion, the likes of which they had never known. Daniel had never been away that long, and so his family was bursting with excitement that he had finally returned. After they had said good-bye to Jeanne, they headed for home.

Exactly one week later, both the Rubin and Raines families were at the Rubin residence. Ken and Ed were standing over the barbecue, arguing over just how burnt the chicken should be. Lillian and Marie were enjoying some much-deserved rest under the nice late spring sun. And, it being an unusually warm day, Gabe, Shane, and Robert were in the pool, challenging each other to diving contests. Daniel and Jake were nowhere to be found, however.

"You know this was their day, they set it up," Lillian said.

"They'll be here," said Marie. "Maybe they got held up."

"Well, I hope they get back before lunch is ready," Lillian replied. "I'm really excited for this surprise."

As Lillian finished her sentence, Daniel and Jake came out through the sliding door onto the deck. And behind them walked two beautiful young women that neither mother had ever seen before.

"This is Jamie," Daniel said, bringing forward a beautiful brunette with lightly freckled cheeks and gorgeous blue eyes.

"And this is Liz," said Jake, standing next to a small blonde with a beautiful smile.

The three boys ran up, still dripping wet from the pool.

Gabe extended his hand and said, "Hello, I'm …"

"Gabe?" Jamie finished the sentence for him, shaking his hand.

"And you're Robbie, right?" Liz said.

"And this little guy must be Shane! Wow, he's so cute!" Jamie said, to which Shane scowled. "In a rugged, manly sorta way!" Jamie finished, laughing.

The three boys dried off, and as they sat down at the table lunch was served. There was grilled chicken, burnt somewhere in between the taste of the two chefs, then corn on the cob prepared on the grill. The menu also included barbecued baby back ribs, and barbecued steak on a stick. The last item on the table was shrimp that had been prepared inside on the wok because Shane was allergic.

"So where's the rest of it?" Jake laughed.

"Well, it is only lunch," Ed replied with a smile.

Lunch was delicious, and Jamie and Liz blended in perfectly. By the end of the meal the three younger boys loved them, and all four parents were suitably impressed. Mostly they were impressed at how their sons acted with the girls, more like themselves than ever before. They were happy for Daniel and Jake, and for the girls, who also seemed extremely comfortable in this new setting.

On the Wednesday of the following week, Ken and Lillian had a dinner date with Ed and Marie, so all five boys decided to get together at the Rubin residence, their usual hangout. While Daniel and Jake went to pick up pizza for dinner, the three younger boys sat and watched television. They always enjoyed nice, fun evenings when it was just the five of them. Daniel and Jake were a lot of fun to hang out with, and could always think of interesting, amusing ways to fill up the time. On this particular night Daniel had promised them a very special surprise, to be had after dinner. Gabe was hoping it was cake, Shane hoped it was a video game, and Robert was in the mood for some ice cream.

So after they had finished dinner, Shane said, "What about the surprise?"

"Oh, it isn't here yet," Daniel responded. "Just relax, we'll tell you when it is time."

So the younger boys went back to the couch to absorb themselves in some more television. When Jake finally told them they were going outside to get the surprise, they were too engrossed in the television to even notice. Daniel and Jake walked through the den into the backyard. The sliding glass door allowed them to still see what the boys were watching. Then, moments after the door closed, a bright blue light lit up the backyard. Seconds later a green one followed it. This was enough to attract even Shane's attention, and they ran to the door. Suddenly it slid back, and two swordsmen in black armor walked into the room.

"Dan, Jake?!?" Shane exclaimed.

"Yeah, it's us," Daniel said with his usual warm smile.

"Why are you dressed like that?" asked Robert.

"It's the latest fashion," Jake said. "No, actually in Paris we found these swords. Every time we touch them we become stronger, faster, and our clothes change to look like this."

"That's amazing!" Gabe said. "How much stronger and faster?"

"Well, watch this," said Daniel, moving into the living room. He still had on his signature smile as he lightly pushed himself off the ground. He floated up, and touched the twenty-foot-high ceiling.

"Awesome!" Shane said after Daniel had lightly touched down on the floor once again.

Robert had a troubled look on his face. "What's the matter, Robbie?" Jake asked.

"Well, I hate to tell you," Robert replied, "but those disguises kinda suck. I can still tell it's you."

"They aren't really disguises," Daniel replied. "The masks are to protect our eyes. And for people who don't know us this will work fine. And as for people that do know us, well they would know us no matter how good our disguises were."

"Oh, OK," said Robert.

"That must be why you're telling us about this now, before you do anything with it," said Gabe, his head cocked slightly to the side, as it always was when he knew he was right.

"Exactly," said Jake. "And we wanted you three to be the first that knew about us."

"So you are going to tell the mothers?" Gabe asked.

"Eventually," said Daniel, rubbing his head. "They're going to kill us when they find out, though, so I think we'll wait a little while."

"In any case, we told you guys now for two reasons," said Jake. "The first is that we were told to tell you."

"By who?" Robert asked.

"By me," said a voice.

"Who said that?" Shane asked, looking around quickly.

"I did," said the voice, taking the shape of Mercury.

"This is Mercury," said Jake. "He is the one who created these swords. Now his ghost is their guardian."

"He's been teaching us how to use our new powers. And now that we can finally crack the boulder in half, he told us we could tell you," Daniel added.

"What boulder?" Shane asked.

"Long story," Jake explained.

"Oh, cool," said Gabe. "Now what's the other reason?"

"Other reason for what?" Daniel asked quizzically.

"You said there were two reasons why you told us," replied Gabe. "What's the second reason?"

"Oh, right," said Daniel, laughing. "Well, actually we were hoping you could help us out with something."

"Doesn't really look like you need our help with much of anything," Robert said.

"Well, actually we were having a bit of a hard time coming up with a name," Jake said.

"A name?" Shane asked.

"Yeah, for us as a superhero team," Jake answered. "Teams always have cool names. We figured maybe you guys could help."

"We would be delighted to!" said Shane with a smile.

The three younger boys huddled together, talking in whispers so that only they could hear. They seemed to be arguing, though Daniel and Jake could not hear what about. Daniel and Jake began to grow impatient, as the process was taking much longer than expected. Finally, after what seemed like ages of whispering and waiting, the three younger boys walked back to them.

"We've got it," said Shane, the self-appointed spokesman of the group. "We have decided on a name for you guys as a team. Since those look like medieval swords, and you two are wearing forms of armor, we think this name will do fine. You will be called the Knights."

"The Knights," said Mercury. "That is a fine name!"

"Wow, that's really good, kinda catchy," said Daniel.

"I'm definitely a fan," Jake agreed, nodding his head.

"Well, then it is settled," Mercury said. "Now, are the Knights ready for battle?"

"You better believe it!" said Daniel, drawing his sword.

"Finally, we can use what we've learned," said Jake, drawing his as well.

They crossed their swords, and then raised them into the air, finally ready to take on the world.

Chapter 4

Saving the Day

The rest of that night was spent just as all times were when those five were together. The television was always on, but they rarely actually watched it. For the most part they chased each other around the house, wrestling and practicing moves on each other while Roxy barked her head off at them. She was not very accepting of their physical games. They even went into the basement and played dodge ball: a demanding sport, both physically and mentally. Then, when they finally got tired, they collapsed in front of the television for a few minutes. When they got their strength back, they would start all over again. But the younger boys still had school, so Jake and Robert left at ten o'clock.

While the younger boys were at school, Jake and Daniel had plenty to keep them busy. They went to Ju-Jitsu four nights a week, because Ju-Jitsu had made them into the people they had become. Also, the people at their dojo were their friends, and a big part of their lives.

They still trained hard with Mercury, because, as Mercury said, "You never know how tough your opponents will be." But they had been back nearly two weeks already, and had not been needed once. They were becoming upset that they had yet to show the world their abilities. Then it happened.

Exactly one week after they told Gabe, Robert, and Shane about the swords, Jake and Daniel got up early to go into the City with their girlfriends. To a true New Yorker, "the City" refers to Manhattan. Going into the City had actually been Jamie's idea. They had not seen Jeanne since getting back to the United States, and so Jamie decided they could meet her in the City. Daniel decided to bring Ryan, so that Jeanne wouldn't feel left out. He figured that they might hit it off, so he sneakily decided to set them up. The ride to Jamaica was only about a half hour long, and that was where they met Jeanne. Jeanne got on the train, and joined her friends for the short fifteen-minute ride into Penn Station.

After Jeanne gave them all hugs and sat down, Daniel said, "Jeanne this is Ryan. Ryan, Jeanne."

"Nice to meet you," Jeanne said with a broad smile.

"You, too," Ryan replied, also smiling and blushing slightly.

Liz leaned over to Jake and whispered, "Look at the way they're looking at each other. I think they're smitten!"

Jake gave her the look he always gave when someone said something he did not approve of, with his brow slightly furrowed and lips pressed loosely together. "Smitten?" he asked.

"Yeah!" Liz whispered back. "What?"

"That's a pretty bad word," Jake replied in his sarcastic tone.

"And what word would you use?" Liz asked with a smile.

Jake thought for a second, and then said, "I probably wouldn't."

Liz' theory proved true after they got off the train. Ryan and Jeanne hung back from the other four, taking their time walking along. They seemed to be engaged in a very relaxed and smooth conversation, both smiling the whole time.

"So what does everyone want to do?" Daniel asked as they walked.

"I'm just following today," Jake replied. "It's up to you, dude."

"I agree, I'm in the mood to follow today," Liz agreed.

"You always think of the best things to do anyway," Jamie said.

"OK, that's fine," Daniel said. "Should we ask the lovebirds?"

"Hey, lovebirds!" Jake shouted. "What do you guys want to do?"

Ryan and Jeanne both turned even brighter red than they had been a minute earlier. "I don't care," Ryan barely managed to get out.

"That's so cute!" Liz whispered to the others. "They really are smitten!"

Jake gave another disapproving look as Daniel said, "Yeah, if you ask me it's a little nauseating." Liz smacked him.

"Hey, what are you guys whispering?" Jeanne asked.

"Just how nauseating you two are," Daniel replied. Jamie smacked him. "Er, nothing," he said.

"Sure, whatever," Jeanne replied, smiling.

"OK, well it's a nice day, why don't we just walk around for a while, and then we can have lunch," Daniel suggested.

"Yes, let's," Ryan said, taking Jeanne's hand and looking her in the eyes.

"Yes, let's," Jake said, taking Daniel's hand, mocking Ryan. Jeanne smacked Daniel. "What are you smacking me for?" He asked, rubbing his arm. "Jake said it."

"I don't know, just felt like smacking you is all," Jeanne replied with a shrug.

"Anyone else just feel like smacking me?" Daniel yelled. Jake and Ryan both smacked him, laughing.

Daniel threw up his hands and started to walk away. Jamie caught him by the hand. "Oh, stop being such a big baby, you're not mad," she said, pulling him back and kissing him.

"Eww, get a room!" Jake said. Liz smacked him, and Daniel laughed.

"We have the most romantic boyfriends ever!" Jamie said, obviously being sarcastic.

"All right, let's go already," Daniel said.

They walked around for a while, no particular destination in mind. They talked and laughed, as old friends do. They enjoyed the beautiful weather of the early June day. They told Ryan of some of their adventures in Paris, and he told them what had happened while they were gone. His favorite story of theirs was of the night they met the girls, and the fight inside the club. His already high level of respect for Jamie and Liz went up. He could see why his friends liked them so much. Jeanne shared with him some of the adventures that she had participated in alone, because much of their journey in Paris they spent individually. He walked, riveted to everything she had to say. Yes, he truly was smitten. Soon they found themselves coming up on Central Park. They decided that since they had no particular destination and since it was such a beautiful day, they would have a picnic in the park.

They were sitting and eating for only a few minutes when Mercury's voice exploded inside their heads. "DANGER!!!!"

Daniel and Jake jumped up, looking around feverishly. "Did you guys hear that?" Daniel asked.

"Hear what?" Ryan asked, a confused and concerned look on his face.

"Never mind," Daniel said, his heart still racing.

As they sat back down, Mercury's voice exploded inside their heads once again. "DANGER!!!!" He yelled. "Do not be afraid, I am speaking to you telepathically. You two are the only ones who can hear me. And so that you do not seem insane to your friends, you can answer me in thought."

You scared us! Daniel thought.

"I am sorry," Mercury responded. "I am sending you the shields. They will reach you in around two minutes, so I suggest finding a more discreet place to change."

What's the danger? Jake asked in thought.

"Men with machine guns have taken hostages in a hotel at the downtown edge of the park," Mercury said. "They have made it impossible for the police to get inside. All attempts at negotiation have thus far failed. I think that the Knights would have more luck in convincing the nice men to leave."

Right, we're on it! thought Daniel, a bit of excitement showing. Then he turned to his friends and said, "We'll be right back."

They ran off before the others could say anything, or ask any questions. They had decided to tell the others; they didn't like keeping any secrets from their best friends. But the time wasn't right, not just yet. It is a little difficult to bring up in conversation. No matter what the topic of conversation is, superheroes with thousand-year-old swords never really flows smoothly into it. And certainly there was no way of simply bringing up Mercury. A sorcerer's ghost that had trained them in the middle of a French forest? They thought about how to tell their friends as they ran through the park, and finally spotted the shields.

The shields flew overhead, and then released the swords. The tips were heading straight for their chests, but they turned and avoided them, then grabbed the hilts. The green and blue waves passed over them as soon as they grabbed the swords. By the time they swung the swords onto their backs, they were in full armor, and the scabbards took the swords. Then the Knights launched themselves into the air and called their shields to pick them up. They were off at last to save the day.

As soon as their feet touched the shields, they knew where they were going. It was as though the shields had communicated their destination to them without using any words. They came across the hotel in under a minute. They stopped and surveyed the scene, flying high enough to remain out of sight. There were dozens of police cars, fire trucks, and ambulances in front of the hotel, all with lights on. There was a police officer with a megaphone, attempting to negotiate with the hostage-takers, four of whom were on the eighth floor. They also had two men guarding the lobby, and one on the roof. Mercury had said that all held machine guns, though it would be more accurate to say they were assault rifles, AK-47s, to be exact.

"What are you going to do?" asked Mercury.

I was thinking we could go in through the roof, and work our way down, thought Daniel. *The hostages will be freed before the two on the ground know anything is happening. That way there's no shooting.*

My thoughts exactly, thought Jake.

"Excellent, you two are thinking very sensibly," said Mercury, sounding impressed. "But remember that your strength could kill, and you don't want to kill anyone. So use your abilities as sparingly as possible. Try to find a way to win without fighting."

We'll do our best, thought Jake.

They jumped off the shields and landed on the roof next to the one guard. They were within arms distance of the armed guard, eliminating his firearm advantage. Being close was the only way they could be sure that he would not have a chance to fire his weapon. They were counting on their speed to save them at that range.

"Who are you?" asked the frightened guard.

"We're the Knights," said Daniel. "And we're here to free the hostages."

The guard looked at them, then laughed and said, "Right! You're gonna stop all of us with our guns ... and all you have are those swords and stupid costumes!"

"Well, actually," said Daniel. "We're here to negotiate, and hopefully we won't have to use the swords."

At this the guard let out another chuckle, then raised his weapon to Daniel's chest. Daniel did not budge. He couldn't: he was paralyzed with fear. This was the first time that anyone had pointed a gun at him, and he couldn't help but feel that he might not live to have it happen again. He saw, in slow motion, the tip of the gun being placed against his chest. He saw, in slow motion, the guard begin to pull the trigger. He closed his eyes tight, bracing for the final feeling of his life. He heard the trigger click, and flinched. But nothing happened.

Daniel kept flinching, expecting at any second to feel the explosion against his chest. But it did not come. He slowly opened one eye, then stared wide-eyed in disbelief. He saw Jake, sword tip touching the ground. Then he saw next to the tip the barrel of the gun. Jake had cut the gun in half in the time it took the guard to pull the trigger, so the gun did not fire.

"Thanks," Daniel said, still in awe.

"No problem," Jake replied. "It was like slow motion."

"Yeah, for me, too," Daniel said. "But I thought that was only because I was the one about to be shot."

"Guess not," Jake replied with a shrug.

Through the whole conversation the guard stood, speechless, staring at the butt of his severed gun. He hadn't even seen the guy in the black and blue pajamas move, but there was no doubt that he had cut the gun clean in half. Strange guys in strange pajamas, faster than lightning: they had called themselves the Knights. It was a name that he would not soon forget. He tried to think of a way to warn his friends, but he knew that if he reached for the radio it, too, would be chopped in half, or worse might happen. So he quickly decided that he was in his over his head, and would surrender.

"Wise decision," Jake said after hearing the guard's plan of action.

"And I know just what to do with him," said Daniel, smiling. "Green shield; please take this man slowly down to the farthest police car from the building. That way his friends don't know what happened. As for you, I wouldn't try to escape, or else you'll fall the whole way down," Daniel added, turning to the guard.

The shield responded to what Daniel had said. It quickly flew to the rooftop, stopping next to the guard. It hovered only a foot above the ground, letting Daniel set the confused guard on it. Then the shield floated slowly and steadily down to the police. The officer with the megaphone looked up, and saw two strange characters on the roof. Daniel gave him a quick wave and a smile, then he and Jake moved to the doors that would lead them into the hotel.

There were two stairways in the hotel; both led straight from the basement all the way up to the roof. Then there was one elevator shaft. On the eighth floor, one guard stood in front of each entrance and one in front of the elevator, ensuring that no one could reach the hostages. The fourth hostage-taker on the eighth floor, presumably the leader, was guarding the hostages in room 819. Twenty people were being kept in the one room while the leader of the gang yelled his demands down to the police. He was asking for money, and lots of it, and a miniature school bus for a getaway car. Daniel couldn't believe his ears as he listened to the demands from the north stairwell on the eighth floor. He and Jake would take the guards by the stairs, then meet up at the elevators, as quietly and quickly as possible.

Daniel saw the guard, the assault rifle strapped across his back. He looked almost bored, as though he felt he served no particular purpose. Daniel decided to give him a purpose, however short it was. He walked through the door and stared the guard in the face. The guard, after a split second of complete shock, raised his gun at the green Knight. Once again everything switched to slow motion for Daniel, but this time he did not freeze. Before the guard could fire a single shot, Daniel disarmed him, used a pressure point behind the ear to put the guard to sleep, and carried him toward the elevator.

Daniel saw Jake approaching the elevator as he did. Jake had the other guard in hand, also unconscious. They used the straps from the guards' guns to tie their hands behind their backs. Then they both slowly walked up to the guard standing in front of the elevator. Confusion was the guard's first reaction, and the Knights took advantage of it. The guard (had he been conscious) would have soon found himself tied to the other two guards in such a way that their backs were together, and none of them could move. Then it was time for Daniel and Jake to free the hostages.

"All right, how do you wanna do this?" Daniel asked quietly as they approached room 819.

"Same way that we did the others?" Jake asked.

"I don't know," Daniel said. "There's a possibility that if he sees people with any kind of weapons he'll shoot them. And if we move fast enough to prevent that, we might wind up killing him by accident."

"Hmm." Jake thought for a second. "OK, I have a plan."

"What are you going to do?" Daniel asked as Jake took the sword out of its sheath.

"Just make sure you get the hostages out," Jake whispered as he laid the sword on the ground, transforming back into himself. As he started to walk toward the room, he stopped, turned to Daniel, and said, "Hey, this is cool. Like real superhero spy stuff."

"I know!" Daniel replied. "We rule!"

Jake laughed, and then switched on his poker face. He was good at being serious when he wanted. Daniel had never had that talent; he was always smiling regardless of the situation. Because of this Daniel was glad that Jake was the one having to be serious, while all he had to do was remove the hostages. Jake knocked on the door, and soon had the barrel of an AK-47 pushed into his right nostril. The leader was a very large man, at least six foot five and three hundred pounds. He held the rifle as though it were a pistol. Pushing the gun further up Jake's nose, he snarled, "What do you want?"

"Hi, my name is Jake," Jake said, trying to maintain his composure.

"I will only ask one more time," said the leader, pushing Jake back into the wall behind him. "WHAT DO YOU WANT???"

"I just want to tell you a joke," Jake said with a shrug.

"What?" replied the leader, pushing the barrel of the gun to the point where Jake was in pain. "I don't have time for games."

"All I want is to tell you a joke," Jake said again, delicately removing the barrel of the gun from his nostril and pointing it to the floor. "I'll tell you what. If the joke is bad, you can use that big, shiny gun of yours. But I think it'll be worth your while."

"Are you a cop?" the leader asked warily.

"Do I look like a cop?" Jake asked, indicating his jeans and T-shirt. "Besides, I haven't heard many cops try to tell jokes."

"Fine, but make it quick," the leader said, slinging the gun across his back.

The leader had pushed Jake far enough out of the room that Daniel could sneak in, and start freeing the hostages. Jake saw Daniel enter the room, but he knew it would probably take his friend a long time to get all of the hostages out. So he began to tell the longest, and most annoying, joke in his arsenal.

"OK," he began. "So it's a boy's fifth birthday. He asks his father for a gift, and the father gives him fifty pink ping-pong balls. The boy says, 'Daddy, what's with the ping-pong balls?' The dad says, 'I'll tell you on your twenty-fifth birthday.' The next year his birthday comes and this time the father gives him a hundred pink ping-pong balls. He says to his father, 'Dad I can't wait for my twenty-fifth birthday. Why are you giving me these ping-pong balls?'" Jake paused for a moment, looking to see how Daniel was doing removing the hostages.

"What happened next?" asked the leader, really getting into the joke.

"Right," said Jake, returning to his mission. "Where was I? Oh, right. So the father replies, 'I'll tell you on your twenty-fifth birthday.' So the years go by and every year the boy's father gives him more pink ping-pong balls. For his fifteenth birthday, his father gives him one million pink ping-pong balls." He looked at Daniel, who was almost done freeing the frightened and confused hostages. So Jake decided to finish the joke that could be as long as he wanted it to be.

"All right," Jake said. "So the boy's twenty-fifth birthday comes. By this time he has, like, seventeen million pink ping-pong balls. But he's excited, because this is the day he's been waiting for all his life. He finally gets to find out why his father had been giving him the pink ping-pong balls. Then, when his father is on the way to finally clear up the mystery, he gets into a car crash and dies."

The leader looked at Jake, dumfounded. Daniel, having freed the last of the hostages and only sitting around to hear the end, smacked his hand against his forehead at the stupidity of his best friend's joke. The leader heard the noise and wheeled around. He saw what was going on, and wheeled back around angrily, feeling betrayed by his own jester. Then he turned to Daniel and raised his gun. Before the man could fire the weapon Jake landed a punch to his jaw, momentarily stunning the man. A moment was all that Jake needed as he followed up, knocking the man unconscious.

Jake picked up his sword, and once again the blue wave turned him into the blue Knight. Daniel walked up, and Jake said to him, "And you said my jokes weren't useful."

"Oh, no, that's not true," Daniel replied. "I said your jokes weren't funny. There's a difference."

"Sure, change your story," Jake answered. "Whatever. Let's finish this, shall we?"

"We shall," Daniel replied with a nod.

They escorted the hostages down the two staircases, and then told them to wait inside the stairwells. They waited and watched as the two downstairs guards heard the elevator open. Confused, they walked up to it, ready to fire, thinking that a silly hostage had escaped and was using the elevator to get to freedom. They were amazed to find their four friends from upstairs tied together, unconscious. Then, suddenly, they both felt blades raised to their throats.

"Drop the guns," said Daniel.

They did as they were told, and the Knights brought the six culprits outside to the police. They were followed by all of the hostages, running to safety. The officer with the megaphone ran over to them.

"How did you two … ?" the amazed officer asked.

"Carefully," Jake replied with a laugh.

"Well, thank you!" the officer stammered.

"Don't mention it," Jake responded.

"Who are you guys, anyway?" the officer asked.

"We're the Knights," said Daniel. Then he and Jake launched themselves into the air. The shields picked them up, and they were off.

"Excellent job," Mercury's voice came into their heads, softer than before. "I couldn't have done better myself."

Thank you, Daniel thought. *Though that's not much of a compliment, considering the fact that you are a ghost.*

"You know what I meant. Now go, change back, and rejoin your friends. They'll be worried about you," Mercury told them.

Oh, about that, thought Jake. *I was thinking we should tell them tonight, and our parents, too.*

"Why's that?" Mercury asked.

Well, because this whole thing will probably be in the newspapers tomorrow and on the news tonight. They will see our pictures and know immediately that it's us. So rather than try to hide it, and have them find out from someone else, I think we should tell them so they can hear it from us, first, Jake thought.

Yeah, I agree, thought Daniel.

"Very well," said Mercury. "You make a good point. You should indeed tell them tonight."

They had the shields drop them off in the same place as they had been picked up. Then they put the swords down and changed back into their normal selves. The whole rescue had taken only fifteen minutes, so they assumed their friends would still be waiting for them.

As they approached the others, Jeanne stood up and yelled, "Where in the world have you two been?"

"Bathroom emergency," said Daniel.

"You're kidding, right?" Jeanne asked incredulously.

"Actually, yes," said Daniel. "But don't worry; we will explain everything after dinner tonight."

"Dinner?" Ryan asked.

"Yeah, you're all invited to my house for dinner," replied Daniel. "Jake and I have a surprise for everybody, so we suggest that you accept the invitation."

"You sound so stuffy!" Jake said. "Just go for dinner, trust us."

"All right, you convinced me," Jamie said.

"Yeah, sounds good to me," Liz agreed.

"Well, not like I have anything better to do," Ryan announced with a smile and two thumbs up. "You can count on me."

"Fine, fine," Jeanne said. "Me, too."

"Excellent," Jake said. "I'm gonna call my family and tell them to meet us at Dan's house."

"Yeah, I should probably tell my family, too," Daniel said.

"You didn't ask your family?" Jamie asked, amazed.

"Not yet, but it'll be OK," Daniel replied. "Now I'm gonna go make that phone call."

Daniel and Jake spoke to their parents, who were as bewildered as their friends. They couldn't imagine what the surprise could be, which was strange because their eldest sons almost never kept secrets from anybody. After speaking to the parents, the six friends walked around Manhattan. The afternoon was not as exciting as the morning, and they soon found themselves on the train home. Daniel and Jake were the only ones talking on the train ride. The others sat and wondered what the surprise could be. Jamie, who was normally excellent at reading Daniel, could not figure out what her boyfriend was hiding.

Daniel had sounded so sincere on the phone that as soon as Lillian Rubin hung up with him, she began preparations. He had pleaded with her not to make dinner extravagant, he was hoping for pizza but he understood if Chinese food was waiting for them instead. Still though, she had to quickly get the house in order for the guests. Ken was even on his way home from work to help. But neither of them had any clue as to what the surprise could be. When Gabe got home from school, she decided to ask him if he knew anything about it.

"Surprise?" Gabe asked. "What surprise?"

"I don't know, I was hoping you'd tell me," Lillian responded.

"I know nothing of any surprise, and don't bother asking Shane or Rob, they don't know, either," Gabe replied, smiling.

"You are such a liar!" Lillian laughed. "So what is it?"

"If I told you it wouldn't be a surprise," Gabe said. "Besides, it isn't even my surprise to tell, so that wouldn't be fair to Dan."

"I can't believe you would keep a secret from your own mother," Lillian said, jokingly.

"You'll find out tonight," Gabe said, and proceeded to help his mother clean up.

Later that evening, the entire Rubin family, as well as the entire Raines family were eating dinner, with Jamie, Liz, Ryan, and Jeanne. It was a very leisurely dinner, with talking and laughing, and even some singing by Jake. He wasn't very good, but that never stopped him from hitting those high notes. Finally they were finished, and they all moved into the den and sat on the couches. There wasn't enough room, so Gabe, Robert, and Shane sat on the floor.

"OK, we have an announcement to make," said Daniel.

"But we need to go get something first," Jake added, and they both stepped out of the room.

"OK, so what do you guys think it is?" Ken asked.

"Maybe they got tattoos?" asked Ryan.

"Where did that come from?" Shane asked. "But no, that's not it."

"Maybe they are proposing to the girls?" Jeanne asked. Jamie and Liz blushed, and suddenly became very worried.

"Um, I don't think so," Gabe shook his head, and the girls breathed an audible sigh of relief.

Just then, the door opened, and then shut again. They heard slow footsteps, and then saw the Knights at the doorway to the den. They were wearing their full armor, and their swords were at the backs. Mercury, the silver ghost, was with them.

"Guys, Halloween isn't for, like, five months," Ken said.

"Those aren't Halloween costumes, Dad," Shane said. "They're the Knights!"

"Oh, OK," said Ken. "Who are the Knights?"

"Well, we use our incredible powers to fight for justice and happiness," said Daniel.

"And how much does that pay?" Ed asked, laughing.

"Hey, this is real!" Jake said. "We freed hostages from gunmen in a hotel this morning!"

"Well I don't like that at all," Lillian said. "It sounds way too dangerous."

"Actually, madam," said Mercury, speaking for the first time that night, "they are well beyond the point where they could be hurt by guns."

"Who are you?" Marie asked, annoyed.

"My name is Mercury," Mercury replied. "I am the creator and guardian of the swords. I trained these young men after they found the swords two months ago in Paris."

"Well, to me it sounds like you are putting these boys in danger, and I don't like it," Lillian said.

"The world will need these boys soon, so it is not entirely up to you, madam," Mercury said.

"Not up to me?" Lillian yelled. "I am Daniel's mother, and that means that I without a doubt have a say in this!"

"I do not mean to be rude," Mercury said.

"Well, I have to tell you that whether you mean to be or not, you are being extremely rude," Marie said, picking up where Lillian left off. "These are our sons, and even if they are all grown up we don't want to see them in any danger. We are invested in this whether you like it or not, because it affects us. So don't you dare tell us that it is not up to us!"

"Mom, please, we're OK," Jake said.

"Yeah, our powers are incredible," Daniel added. "And we are training everyday to become even better."

"Well, I won't allow it," Lillian said.

"You know we didn't even have to tell you," Daniel replied. "If you read comic books, most superheroes don't tell their loved ones. But we didn't want to keep any secrets from you. So we told you. And now you tell us we can't use the amazing power we've been blessed with to help others? Maybe those comic book heroes had the right idea."

Lillian paused for a moment, and then sighed. "No, you're right. You didn't have to tell us, but you did. I appreciate your honesty. What do you think, Marie?"

"I guess their honesty does speak volumes," Marie agreed. "And if they were able to take out an entire hotel of armed men they can obviously take care of themselves. Just be careful, OK?"

"We always are," said Jake.

"Thank you!" said Daniel, giving his mother a kiss on the cheek.

"So now when you see us on the news tonight you won't be surprised," Jake said.

"We're looking forward to it," said Lillian.

As all things must come to an end, the party ended a short while later. Jeanne had taken the train to meet them, but Ryan offered to drive her back home. She eagerly agreed.

"Those two are going to wind up getting married," Daniel said as he and Jake walked to the car with Jamie and Liz.

Liz was staying at Jamie's house for the evening. They had been best friends since childhood, and often spent nights at each other's houses. So Daniel and Jake went together to drive them back.

"So did you find the swords before or after you met us?" Jamie asked.

"The same night, actually," said Daniel. "Soon after we dropped you guys off at the Métro."

Jake squeezed Liz's hand in the back seat and said, "That was a great night."

"Yeah, some birthday for you!" Liz said.

"Seriously," Jake agreed. "I can't wait to see what I get next year!"

"Jamie, what's wrong?" Daniel asked from the driver's seat where he could see her hanging her head, and off in her own world.

"Nothing," she replied.

"Oh, just tell me," Daniel answered.

"Well it's just that you've been hiding this from us for two months!" Jamie finally answered.

"Not exactly," Daniel said. "I mean this was a pretty big thing, it needed to be said at the right time. Besides, we had to tell our brothers first."

"But still, you kept a secret from us for two months," Jamie insisted.

"We kept this secret from everybody," Daniel said, trying to prevent the disaster he knew was happening.

"Well, what other secrets are you keeping?" Jamie asked. "How do we know you aren't hiding anything else from us?"

"Because we aren't," Daniel replied. "Don't you trust me?"

"Well, I did, but I don't know if I should now that I know you've been keeping something this big from me," Jamie said, pulling her hand away from Daniel's.

"Please don't be like this," Daniel said. "Could you imagine if I told you right away that I was some sort of superhero? You would have been freaked out! Besides, if we told you right away we'd never know if you guys were with us just because of that. I especially would have been paranoid about that for the rest of my life. But now we know that you two are the most incredible girls that we've ever met. You probably have stronger characters than either of us heroes. You, Jamie, are the only girl I have ever met where, the more time I spend with you, the more time I want to spend with you. So we told you as soon as we thought we could, for our safety as well as yours. OK?"

As Jamie took his hand again, Daniel said, "You know we wouldn't even have found the swords if it wasn't for you two."

"Why do you say that?" Liz asked.

"Well, Jeanne and the others left the club early that evening," Jake answered. "We stayed late because we had met you two. Any earlier and we wouldn't have been around to help the woman and her son, and then we wouldn't have found the swords."

"Yep," said Daniel, squeezing Jamie's hand. "It's destiny."

"I like destiny," Jamie said, squeezing back. "But Dan, I have to ask you something. Isn't this dangerous?"

"What, holding hands while driving? Probably," Daniel answered, smiling.

"Funny," she replied sarcastically. "You know what I mean."

He looked at her and smiled, then looked back at the road. "No. You heard what Mercury said. The Knights are at a level far beyond average people."

"A little conceited, are we?" Jamie smiled.

"Not us, the Knights," Daniel smiled back.

"You are the Knights," Jamie responded.

"Not without the swords," said Daniel. "Without the swords we're nothing. But with the swords we can handle anything that comes our way."

She looked at him, the concern still showing behind her eyes. "All right, then, do your best. You show those bad guys who's in charge!"

"Will do," he replied.

As he finished talking he pulled up to her house. The girls gave their boys a kiss good-bye, then got out and walked toward the door. Daniel watched them enter the front door as Jake climbed into the front seat. Once they were inside, Daniel pulled away.

After a minute of driving, Jake asked, "What's on your mind?"

"Maybe we should have told them sooner," Daniel replied.

"No, weren't you listening to yourself? You were right," Jake answered. "There's something else though, isn't there?"

"Well, we're much stronger than the guys we faced today, right?" Daniel asked.

"Apparently," Jake shrugged his shoulders. "So much so that if we used our full power we'd kill them."

"Well, the fact that we are so powerful worries me," Daniel said.

"Well, if we hold back we won't kill people," Jake replied.

"No, that's not it," Daniel said. "We are so far beyond 'normal' people that we can't even be hurt by people with guns. Yet Mercury still has us train harder, always trying to get stronger."

"So what are you thinking?" Jake asked.

"That maybe Mercury isn't training us to fight people like that," Daniel answered mysteriously.

"You mean … ?" Jake began.

"Yeah," Daniel interrupted. "I think that Mercury is training us to fight against a different enemy. One as powerful as us. Or … even more powerful."

Chapter 5

A New Enemy

"Now the game truly begins," Mercury said to himself as he watched Daniel and Jake pull away from Jamie and Liz's apartment.

He began the long journey overseas that would commence his final plan. He hated doing things this way, hated the fact that he had to be neutral. But he was guide and guardian to the swords, not to their holders. That meant that he had to make sure the swords wound up in their rightful places regardless of how much he liked, or disliked, the vessels that brought them there.

He knew exactly what was going to happen, and how it needed to happen as well. That was his curse: knowing what would happen, yet being completely unable to change or prevent it. If he interfered on either side's behalf he would change the outcome, which absolutely could not happen. If the future changed, the world might be in even greater danger. So he could not interfere, and that fact had been eating him up inside for the past thousand years, ever since his powers of foresight had been amplified at death. Even though Mercury saw an outcome, he could not be sure that that was what would actually happen, for that is the nature of foresight. Just knowing the future could change it. So he had to be extra careful. It must end as he saw.

"Funny," he thought. "Most people worry about the future because they don't know what it will bring. I worry about it because I do know what it will bring."

He smiled at the strange irony of life, but the smile quickly faded from his lips. He could not bear to think of the loss that they would have to go through. Before this adventure was over, each of the main players would feel the pain of loss in some way or another. He felt especially bad for Daniel, who would have to suffer the most. He saw once again the vision that he had suffered through for the past millennium. He saw Daniel, stripped of his power, far away from all of his loved ones, dropped to one knee. He saw the demon standing in front of Daniel, poised to strike. He saw Daniel, head always held so high, drop his gaze. Then the vision went black.

"The balance must be maintained, for the good of the earth," Mercury said to himself with a deep sadness.

The next morning, Gabe and Shane woke up at 5:45 a.m., their normal routine for a school day. They would walk Roxy in the backyard together, then sit and eat their breakfast while watching cartoons. Then they would shower, get dressed, and wait for their buses to come. That particular morning, after walking the dog, they put on the six o'clock news instead of cartoons. They had to suffer through a few minutes of regular news before they found what they had been looking for.

"And in other news," said the news anchor, "in an incredible scene, two lone men, armed only with swords, stopped seven gunmen and freed the hostages that had been taken inside a New York City hotel. Even more impressive is the fact that the two men escorted all of the gunmen, tied up yet otherwise unharmed, to the local authorities. We have exclusive footage of their triumphant exit from the scene."

A video then showed Daniel and Jake in their armor walking out behind the hostages. Daniel was carrying a young child, whom he passed off to her mother once they were out of the building. Jake was escorting the gunmen out to the police. Gabe and Shane cheered out loud when they heard Daniel speak the name that they had made up to the world. Then the two Knights leapt up into the air so high that the camera lost them in the sun. The video stopped, and the feed returned to the newsroom.

"Just who are these Knights?" the anchor asked her viewer audience. "Are they friend or foe? Are they our heroes or our nightmares? Will we be seeing them again? One thing is certain, only time will tell. Our next story …"

Gabe turned off the TV as Shane said, "Wow, I can't believe they were really on TV!"

"Yeah, it's awesome," Gabe said.

"Should we wake Danny up?" Shane asked.

"Nah, he'll find out," Gabe said. "Besides, he wouldn't want us to wake him up this early anyway."

"I guess you're right," Shane agreed. "Hey did you hear him say the name we gave them?"

"Yeah," Gabe replied. "And did you see how high they jumped? People probably thought that they just flew away."

"Man, it would have been so cool to be them right then," Shane said. "I wish I could be a Knight."

"Me, too," Gabe said. "But we can't. Maybe we can help them out, though. I mean, even superheroes need help sometimes, right?"

"Yeah!" Shane responded. "That's a really good idea."

"Cool, and you can start helping by going in the shower first," Gabe replied with a smile.

"How would that help them?" Shane asked, puzzled.

"It wouldn't," Gabe replied. "But it would help me by letting me watch more TV."

"That's not fair!" Shane said, unwilling to stand for the injustice. "You take longer anyway, and have to leave earlier."

"Fine, fine, fine," Gabe said, lifting himself from the couch.

Far across town, there was another younger brother watching the news. Robert had gotten out of bed extra early, nearly an hour before his normal time. Groggy and missing his bed, he sat down in front of his television. By the time the segment was over, however, Robert had more energy than he could ever remember having that early in the morning. His brother really was a hero, and it was even better than Mercury had said. He rushed through getting ready, and waited very impatiently for his bus. By the time he got to school, Gabe was already at his locker waiting.

"Hey," Gabe said as Robert walked up.

"Wassup?" Robert replied.

"So did you see the news?" Gabe asked quietly.

"Yeah, isn't it awesome?" Robert replied. "They really kicked some butt."

"I know," Gabe agreed. "But the most amazing thing is that they were able to kick butt without fighting at all."

"Yeah, they must be really good," Robert said. "I want to be that good."

"Me, too," Gabe answered, thinking. "Hey, I know! Why don't we train with them? Even though we don't have swords I'm sure we can take part in their training. And that way if they ever need any help, we'll be there for them."

"That's a really good idea," Robert replied. "I really like that. Shane, too?"

"Well, it wouldn't be fair to say he couldn't train with us," Gabe said. "Though I think he's a bit small to help out in a real situation."

"OK, so he just won't come on any missions or anything," Robert said.

Just then, Robert blushed. Without even looking, Gabe knew what had happened. The Gorgeous Girl had walked by. She always smiled at Robert, but he just blushed and looked away. She probably thought he hated her.

"Go talk to her," Gabe said.

"You go talk to her," Robert replied, blushing even more.

"I'm not the one who's in love with her."

"I … I can't talk to her," Robert sighed.

"Why not?" Gabe asked. By this time the Gorgeous Girl had long since walked away.

"Hey, why are you coming down on me?" Robert turned the conversation around. "I don't see you dating, even though there are plenty of girls who like you."

"What girls?" asked Gabe.

"Rachel, Christine, Lauren, Catherine," Robert started.

"I didn't know they liked me," Gabe said, rubbing his neck.

"Yes, you did," Robert said, smiling. "You were just afraid to ask them out. So I'm not the only one."

Their minds were overflowing for the rest of that day. First, they thought of the newscast, and the many to come involving their heroic brothers. Then they thought of how incredible it would be to be the heroes themselves. They imagined themselves looking at all the news cameras, all calm and cool, then leaping effortlessly off into the sky. Then they imagined themselves sweeping young ladies off their feet—any young lady they wanted, because naturally everyone would love them. And so they daydreamed the day away, hardly paying attention to school at all.

Shane, however, did not have such an easy day. When he got home, Daniel was sitting at the kitchen table reading a newspaper article about the Knights.

"Do I look fat in this picture?" Daniel asked Shane jokingly. Shane did not smile. "You all right?" Daniel asked.

"I'm fine," Shane said through a sob as he ran up to his room.

Daniel followed him, not entirely convinced. "What's up?" he asked, walking into Shane's room.

"Nothing! Go away!" Shane said, his face in the pillow.

Daniel sat down on Shane's bed, then put his hand on Shane's back. Shane peeked out from under his pillow to see Daniel smiling at him. He sat up, dried his eyes, and blew his nose. He knew that no matter what happened he could always talk to his brothers, especially Daniel. Daniel somehow always knew what to say to make him feel better. So he started telling Daniel about his day.

"I got in trouble today," Shane said.

"What? What happened?" asked Daniel.

"Well, I told you about the kid who keeps pushing me around?" asked Shane.

"Yeah, the big ugly kid whose mother is the principal?" Daniel replied.

"Yeah, that kid, Melvin," said Shane. "Well, I was coming back from the bathroom when he came out of his mother's office. I walked by, trying to just ignore him. But he stole my hall pass right out of my hand and ripped it up."

"What? Then what happened?" asked Daniel.

"Well, I just went to walk back to my class," said Shane. "But he got in my way. I asked him to please move, but we wouldn't. Then he pushed me."

"He pushed you?" Daniel asked. "Did anyone see this?"

"No," said Shane through a lump in his throat.

"Oh, that sucks!" Daniel replied. "Then what happened?"

"Well, he went to push me again," said Shane. "But I didn't let him. I moved out of the way, then lightly took him down. That's when his mother came out of her office. She just saw him on the floor and me standing over him with no hall pass. And then he started crying saying how mean I was and how I'd just walked up and pushed him. She wouldn't listen to anything I said, she wouldn't even let me go back to my class to have my teacher tell her I had a hall pass. She just kept me in her office for the rest of the day. I didn't even get lunch."

"WHAT?" Daniel exclaimed. "How could she do that?"

"What should I do?" Shane asked, tears in his eyes.

"I think you should tell Mom and Dad," said Daniel. "They always seem to know what to do about this stuff."

"Can't you just go talk to her as the Green Knight?" Shane asked.

"Oh, yeah, I can see the headlines in tomorrow's paper," Daniel said with a smile. 'Knights Threaten Elementary School Principal.' I'm looking for PR, but not quite like that. Somehow I don't think that would go well with the whole hero bit. Trust me. Talk to Mom and Dad. You only have a little over a month left, and it certainly can't get any worse."

"All right," said Shane at last.

"Now you know what I think? I think we should play some football," said Daniel.

"All right," said Shane again, smiling.

They ran downstairs, and then with Gabe, went out to throw a football around on their front lawn. None of them actually played football; that was Robert's game. But still they enjoyed it, and enjoyed being outside on a warm, sunny day. But more than anything, they loved being together.

As they were throwing the football around, Gabe said, "Hey, Dan, we'd like to ask you something."

"What's up?" Daniel asked.

"Well, we know that you and Jake train almost every day," explained Gabe, "and the three of us wanna train with you."

"Really?" Daniel asked. "It's not easy, you know. Two intense hours."

"We know," said Gabe. "But we want to. And besides, me and Rob figure we could help. Shane probably couldn't help, he's too small."

"Am not!" Shane answered.

"Guys, chill," Daniel said. "I'm not putting any of you in danger like that. I'd love to have you train with us, but it's not up to me."

Just then, Mercury appeared. "Hello," he said.

"Good timing," said Daniel.

"Mercury, can we train with them?" asked Gabe.

"Well, it's long, grueling intense training," Mercury replied. "Think you can handle it?"

"Absolutely," said Shane. "We may not be as strong as they are, but we are definitely just as tough."

"Well, what do you think, Dan?" Mercury asked.

"It's fine with me," said Daniel.

"Me, too," came Jake's voice. He was linked to the conversation through Mercury.

"Then it's settled," said Mercury. "As of tonight, the Knights have three new training partners."

"All right!" shouted Gabe and Shane in unison.

That night, their training began. The younger boys could not quite keep up with Daniel and Jake, but then they were not really expected to. They did the best they could, which was quite impressive. Even though their brothers were bordering on superhuman, they were almost as strong and fast. And they did help the Knights, in a few ways. First they helped develop a new training technique: four against one. Daniel and Jake would switch off being the one, then the other four would attack.

The one would have to defend himself for a certain amount of time. Within a month, they all had faster reflexes, and were stronger, faster, and more agile than ever.

One day Daniel and Jake were sitting around when they decided to turn on the news to see if any of their stories were still running. They had helped the police on a drug bust a few days earlier, and figured that might still be on the news. Generally their stories ran for at least a few days, or until they helped out again.

"Now a special report," said the anchor. "Heroes gone bad. In this security video from a Manhattan bank, the Knights, beloved heroes, are seen robbing the bank, then brutally murdering all those inside."

A black and white video came on the screen. It showed two men, wearing armor identical to theirs, walking out of the bank, stepping over bodies as they left. The two men were very obviously not Daniel and Jake, but still they had to wonder at the armor, and the swords at their backs.

The anchor came back on after the video stopped. "Police are now searching for the Knights. If you have any information regarding their whereabouts or regarding this incident, please notify local law enforcement."

Daniel turned off the TV. "What was that?" he asked.

"I ... I don't know," said Jake.

"Well, it wasn't us, was it?" Daniel asked. "They didn't look like us. But those swords ... and that armor?"

"I know, it's really weird," Jake said. "Could they be imposters?"

"Unfortunately, that is not the case," said Mercury, as always, popping up unexpectedly.

"Then who are they?" Jake asked.

"They are the holders of the red and orange swords," said Mercury, with a sigh.

"WHAT? What are you talking about?" cried Daniel.

"What haven't you told us?" asked Jake.

"There aren't two swords," said Mercury. "There are four. I created them nearly a thousand years ago. The son of the man that I created them for began to misuse them, to twist their powers for his own selfish purposes. So I went back to take responsibility for the innocent deaths that my gifts had caused. I fought Ramsey when there was no one else left to fight him. The fight used up all of my life, and so my body died. But my destiny is linked with the destiny of the swords, so my spirit was sent back as their guardian."

"That still doesn't explain the news report," said Jake.

"I'm getting to that part now," said Mercury. "Anyway, I came back in this form, and Ramsey was completely gone. I knew that it would be too dangerous to leave the swords in one spot. So I divided them: two in Paris, two in Rome. For nearly a thousand years I watched over them, and they kept themselves hidden. Then you two came along, and you know what happens from there."

"But what about the other two?" asked Daniel.

"They stayed hidden until one month ago, the very night that you revealed yourselves to your family and friends," said Mercury. "I was there when they were found. The other two do not have good hearts, and so chose to use the swords for their own personal gain."

"And you didn't tell us about them, even though you've known about them for a month already?" Jake asked.

"You did not need to worry about them," said Mercury. "It is your job to protect others, and so you shall. Even if it means protecting them from your own equals."

"Equals?" asked Daniel. "Are they as powerful as us?"

"It is entirely conceivable that they are," Mercury replied. "All four swords are equal in power."

"Wonderful," said Daniel. "But why didn't you tell us about this attack; we could have stopped it."

"Because you needed to know what you were up against," said Mercury.

"Do they know about us?" asked Jake.

"Yes," Mercury said, unable to look Jake in the eye. "I told them everything in hopes that it would change their minds. But it just made their lust for power grow even stronger."

"Wonderful, so we don't even have the element of surprise," said Jake.

"And they could be even more powerful than us," said Daniel, shaking his head.

"Unfortunately, Daniel, that is true," said Mercury. "If you do not know what to expect, expect the worst."

"Great," said Jake.

That evening they told the younger boys everything. The younger boys were shocked, but excited. This meant that they could maybe get swords as well. Daniel and Jake were also mildly excited. They had made several daring rescues, but had never been able to use their power. The thrill of the impending challenge roused their interests. They were worried about the two new swordsmen, but they were looking forward to meeting them.

Whatever the motivation was, they all gave a little extra in their training that night. They came away feeling exhausted, but good. Jamie and Liz couldn't hang out that night, so the five boys decided to hang out together. They had a great night, just spending time watching TV and running around the house as usual.

The next day, Jake was on his way to Daniel's house, stopped at a red light, when Mercury's voice exploded inside his head. "DANGER!!!!"

Jake jumped, then thought to Mercury, *You know it's a good thing I'm stopped, or I woulda gotten into an accident.*

"Sorry," said Mercury. "But the other two are robbing another bank. I'm sending the shields to Daniel's house, get there as soon as possible."

I'll be there in two minutes, Jake thought.

Jake got to Daniel's house just as Daniel was stepping out the door. Jake quickly parked, then ran up to his friend. They did not have any time to speak, because just then the shields flew overhead. They released the swords directly at Daniel and Jake. As always, the two turned out of the way just in time and caught the swords by the hilts, changing into the Knights. Then they leapt into the air, landed on the shields, and were off.

By the time they got to the bank, it was all over. The other two were gone, and they had taken all the cash and valuables hidden within the bank. The reinforced steel doors looked as though they had been torn open. The people in the bank were all dead, and there was no way of telling which way the other two had gone. The Knights walked around, searching for any signs of life. Not a single bystander was left alive. They were about to give up and go home when a police squad car showed up, lights flashing.

"FREEZE!" the officer yelled, crouching behind his car and pointing a shotgun into the bank.

Daniel and Jake came walking out of the bank with their hands in the air. "Let us explain," Daniel said.

"Don't move!" yelled the officer.

"I recognize that voice," Jake whispered to Daniel.

"We just want to talk, please come out," Daniel yelled to the officer, still walking forward.

The Knights heard the trigger being pulled, and dashed off in either direction, the spread just missing them. Then they converged on the squad car, and before the officer had the chance to fire again, Daniel had disarmed him and Jake had a sword to his throat.

"Like we said, we just want to talk," said Daniel, seeing that the officer was the same officer he had spoken to after the hotel incident.

"Want to explain why you killed all of those people?" the officer asked.

"It wasn't us," said Jake.

"Why should I believe you?" the officer asked.

"Because if we killed all of those people, why wouldn't we have just killed you, too?" Jake asked.

"Who was it, then?" the officer asked in response, still not sure what to believe.

"It was two men who have the same powers as us," said Daniel. "But they decided to use that power for their own purposes rather than protecting others. We are here to stop them."

"Then where are they?" asked the officer.

"We don't know; they were gone before we showed up," said Daniel.

Then, Mercury's voice was inside their heads. "Why are you two just standing there?"

They're gone, thought Daniel.

"How did they get away before you got there?" Mercury asked.

They probably used their shields, Jake thought.

"Exactly," said Mercury. "And each shield leaves a distinct trail wherever it goes. Only those who ride the shields themselves can see the trails, which includes you two. So concentrate, and do it quickly before you can't catch them."

Daniel and Jake began to look around, ignoring the confused officer and using their meditation skills to focus only on their task. Soon they no longer heard the noises of the area, or saw the cars whipping by, or even felt the sun beating down on them. Then, as they focused, they began to see what they needed to see: two faint trails, one red, one orange.

"Sorry, we gotta go," said Daniel to the officer as he jumped onto his shield.

They shot off, following the two trails into the distance. The trails were getting stronger, indicating that the heroes were drawing nearer to their opponents. They pushed themselves to full speed as they got closer, doing anything they could to catch their foes.

Soon they could see the two swordsmen in the distance. They didn't even notice that they were being followed themselves. The officer had gotten into his car and was driving behind them. Even though they were going much faster than he was, they did not turn, so, just as a car can follow the movements of an airplane going much faster than itself, the officer was able to follow them. Even so, he was still far behind them when they came up on the other two.

Seeing that they were being followed, the red and orange swordsmen stopped, and turned around. Daniel and Jake had to slam on the brakes to avoid crashing into them. They were staring straight at the other two swordsmen. Their armor was exactly the same, except for the colors. One set was a dark orange, almost brown color. The other was dark maroon red.

The orange one was taller than Jake, with short blond hair. The red one was taller than Daniel but shorter than Jake, and broader and more muscular than either of them. His hair was a reddish color, and his face was lightly freckled. All the same, he looked very menacing, with a face as taut and cold as steel. Then, all of a sudden, he smiled.

"I thought you'd never catch up to us," he said.

"What?" Daniel asked, completely off guard.

"We were riding as slow as we could without falling off. But you caught us, you should congratulate yourselves," said the red villain. Then he pointed to his friend. "By the way this is Hornet. And I am Hellfire. Don't bother introducing yourselves. Green Knight, you are called Daniel, and Blue Knight, you are called Jacob, correct?"

"How did you know that?" Jake asked.

"Mercury, of course," Hellfire replied. "He told us everything about you. It is nice to finally meet you, Knights."

At this point, the officer finally pulled up. He hadn't believed the Knights when they said that there were two others, but now he could see that they had been telling the truth. And, judging by the way they all were standing, or rather hovering, he could see that they were enemies. He sat in his car and waited for what would happen next.

"You know we've been watching you on the news the last couple of weeks," Hellfire said. "We've been keeping a close eye on your story."

"Nice to know we have some fans," said Jake.

"It made us sick," said Hornet, speaking for the first time. "We know you were only helping those people so that they would love you."

"That isn't true," said Daniel. "Whether or not they liked us was never a question."

"Then why would you waste your time with them?" Hellfire asked.

Daniel shot him a sharp look and said, "Because it's the right thing to do. Power exists to protect those who have none."

"That's ridiculous!" Hornet said, laughing.

"The power we have exists for us, and us alone," said Hellfire. "That's why we were chosen."

"What are you saying?" asked Daniel.

"Despite what the sorcerer says, you don't have to help people," Hellfire answered. "Why not help yourselves? Come with us, you can share in our profits!"

"Why would you share with us?" asked Jake. "Wait! I think I know the answer. You're afraid that we will be stronger than you, and that we will be able to stop you. If we stop you, you get nothing."

"Stronger than us?" laughed Hellfire.

"That's right," said Jake. "You knew you couldn't compete with us, so you thought you'd make a 'nice offer' and have us on your side. Then you'd probably just stab us in the back when we turned around. Well, it won't work!"

"You're not stronger than we are," said Hellfire. "No, in all of your exploits you never once displayed any real power. I was trying to give you the easy way out: to serve me. But if you refuse my offer, that makes you my enemies, and then you will know what real power truly is."

"See, I think that true power is knowing how to diffuse a situation without fighting," Daniel said. "And we would never serve you, not in a million years."

"THEN YOU ARE MY ENEMIES!" Hellfire yelled.

With that he shot forward at Daniel. Hornet, following along, shot forward at Jake. Hellfire came at Daniel with a surprisingly powerful and controlled stroke. Daniel blocked it, but as Hellfire shot by he threw another strike. Daniel blocked just in time to keep his head safely secured where it was. Hornet's attack, however, was not as controlled. He took a wild swing at Jake, who simply moved to one side. Hornet was not ready for the miss, and went tumbling off his shield. Jake jumped off his shield after Hornet.

Jake landed to find Hornet pushing himself up. He faced Jake, who was laughing at him. This enraged him even more than falling off his shield, and he swung wildly at Jake, who easily blocked. Jake then kicked at Hornet, but found that his attack had been blocked. Then he felt a sharp crack in the left side of his jaw as Hornet's punch landed. Jake went stumbling back. Hornet, Jake decided, was not a good swordfighter, but was a powerful, polished martial artist. Jake put his sword away, then put his hands up, ready to fight fist to fist.

After Hellfire's first attack, Daniel turned around to face him. He was surprised to see Hellfire jumping off of the shield, heading straight for him. He decided to meet Hellfire, and jumped forward. When they met, their swords clashed, but Daniel managed to throw a kick into Hellfire's chest. Then he called his shield to him, and watched Hellfire fall. The fight was not over, however, and Hellfire's shield caught him. Then he rose up and faced Daniel once again.

"So you can fight," Hellfire said. "Excellent. This may wind up being interesting after all."

"I was just thinking the same thing," Daniel said with a smirk.

Jake had his hands full on the ground. It turned out that Hornet was much more powerful than he looked. He was fast, too, firing punches and kicks quickly at Jake's face. Jake blocked them all, however, waiting for an opening. He saw one, and threw a punch into Hornet's ribs. The punch hit its mark, and sent Hornet to the ground, puffing for breath.

Jake tried to kick Hornet as he was getting up, but Hornet quickly dodged and kicked Jake, sending him back. Hornet followed the kick with a punch, expecting Jake to be stunned. He wasn't, having been kicked harder by his best friend during training. He dodged the punch, and then went on the attack. He hammered his opponent with punches and kicks, sending Hornet back with each strike. Jake finished with a powerful uppercut to Hornet's chin, putting him out on his feet. Hornet was no longer a threat.

While Jake dealt with Hornet, Daniel was going back and forth with Hellfire in the air. They would leap at each other and exchange strikes. Then they would call their shields back to them. At one point, Hellfire came at Daniel while still on his shield. He swung at Daniel's feet, and Daniel jumped just in time. He came down and spun around, only to find Hellfire right behind him. He pushed his feet back so that his chest was parallel to the ground. Hellfire did the same. They spiraled toward the ground, a flurry of fists and steel.

As they were about to hit the ground they pushed off of each other, righted themselves, and flew back up into the air. Immediately they jumped at each other again. This time Hellfire was able to strike Daniel with a kick to the shoulder. Daniel flipped back, calling the shield to catch him. Hellfire was on him again before he even got back to his shield. Hellfire kicked Daniel right in the face, sending him shooting toward the ground. Daniel recovered just in time, and was caught by his shield inches from the ground.

As the fight became more intense, Daniel began to seize the upper hand. He was more acrobatic, and was able to outmaneuver Hellfire in the air. He would simply roll off of Hellfire's punches and kicks, striking

Hellfire when he was most vulnerable. And when Daniel hit, the punches stung, because Hellfire had never been hit that hard before. In a rage, Hellfire leapt at Daniel one last time. He threw his foot out, hoping to kick Daniel before he could make a move. Daniel saw him coming, however, and jumped out to meet him. Using all of his acrobatic ability, he stepped on Hellfire's outstretched left leg with his right foot. Then his left foot pushed off of Hellfire's chest, propelling him into a back flip. As he moved, he crashed his right foot up into Hellfire's chin, sending him spinning toward the ground, nearly unconscious.

The green shield caught Daniel as he came out of his flip. The red shield caught Hellfire just in time, and brought him up to face Daniel once again. Hellfire was recovered, but when he saw Jake rise up next to Daniel, he knew he was defeated. He swept down and picked up Hornet, who was lying on the ground. Then he shot off, with the orange shield following him.

"I will return!" Hellfire yelled as he sped off.

"Well, that was interesting," Daniel said as Jake joined him.

"Certainly," Jake agreed. "Oh, by the way, those were some nice moves. Especially that last one."

"Thanks," said Daniel. "You had some pretty awesome moves yourself. That was the most devastating uppercut I've ever seen. You ready to go?"

"Yeah, let's go home," said Jake.

"Wait," said a voice. They looked down to see the officer calling them.

"Hello, again," Daniel shouted. "Here to arrest us?"

"No," said the officer. "I just wanted to tell you I will take your names off the wanted lists, and give a firsthand report of your innocence to the press."

"Wow, thanks," said Jake. "Hey, what's your name?"

"John Michaels," said the officer. "Sergeant John Michaels."

"Well, thank you, Sergeant John Michaels," said Jake. "I'm glad the Knights can have friends like you."

"And I'm glad that we have friends like the Knights," said Sergeant Michaels, smiling.

Then the Knights shot off toward home. They were pleased with themselves. Their training had paid off, and their abilities were truly marvelous. They couldn't wait for their training that night. They had passed their first real test. But they knew it would not be the last. They were sure that they had not seen the last of the red and orange swords.

Chapter 6

Life

The next morning, Gabe and Robert met at their lockers. Their older brothers had told them about the fight with Hellfire and Hornet, and they could honestly say they were more than a little disappointed. They had been hoping that there were more swords, but that they could have them. The fact that the other two were evil was a major downer. On top of that, they hadn't even been able to help defeat the evil swordsmen. Basically, all of their hopes and dreams had come crashing down in one fell swoop. They were discussing their disappointment when Gorgeous Girl walked up to her locker right across from them.

"Go," said Gabe quietly.

"No, I can't," said Robert.

"Rob, how do you expect to be a Knight if you can't talk to girls?"

"I'll tell you what," Robert said with a new resolve. "I'll talk to her if you talk to a girl that you like."

"OK, sounds good," Gabe answered.

So Robert mustered all of his courage and walked up to her. "Ummm," he mumbled.

"Hi," she said, flashing a dazzling smile directly at him.

"MEROB," he quickly said.

She looked at him, chuckled a little, and then waited for him to continue. When he didn't, she went back to talking with her friends. Robert turned and walked back to Gabe, crushed. Gabe patted him on the back.

"It's OK, it's OK," Gabe said, trying not to laugh.

"Well, that was smooth," Robert said, frowning. "That did not go as planned."

"You really were quite smooth," Gabe said, giving in to his laughter.

"Shut up!" Robert said, pushing him. "You talk to a girl."

Just then the first bell rang, telling them that class was about to start. "Uh-oh, too late," Gabe said with a smile. "Class time."

"No way, you are not getting off that easy."

"Sorry, gotta go," said Gabe, leaving Robert alone.

He was on the couch watching TV with Daniel when Shane came home with a big smile on his face. Daniel had a newspaper in his hand, the front page of which read, "Knights Still Heroes." Then in smaller print it said, "Statement of Sergeant John Michaels, NYPD." Shane walked in to the den and plopped down with them.

"What are you so happy about?" Daniel asked him.

"You remember how you told me to tell Mom and Dad about the bully and his mother?" asked Shane.

"Yeah," Daniel answered.

"Well, I did, and you were right," said Shane with an even broader smile.

"What happened?" asked Gabe.

"Well, Dad went in to talk to her, and you know how he is," said Shane. "She wound up crying right there in the office! Then, even better than that, Dad told the superintendent … and she got fired!"

"What?" Daniel and Gabe asked at the same time.

"Yeah, she's not allowed to come back next year!" Shane said.

"Not a big loss for the school system," Daniel said. "She obviously does not deserve to be working with kids."

"Yeah, apparently I wasn't the only one she was mean to," said Shane. "The superintendent told Dad that she had been notorious for giving kids trouble. Then he agreed with Dad that it was unacceptable, so now she's gone!"

"Congratulations! I'm really happy for you," said Gabe.

"So now you just have one more week of school and you're done?" Daniel asked.

"Not really on subject, but yeah, that's true," said Gabe.

"Well, we were on the subject of school, it was close enough," said Daniel. "Whatever, so starting next week is summer?"

"Yeah!" said Shane.

"Awesome," said Daniel. "Then we can really step up our training. With Hellfire and Hornet out there, we should be at our best."

"Awesome!" Gabe and Shane said at the same time.

"Yeah, it'll be fun," said Daniel as the doorbell rang.

Jamie was there to spend the evening with Daniel, not an unusual occurrence. Most often they went out for the evening together, but this night they had decided to spend the night in. Around six-thirty that evening, Lillian called them downstairs for dinner.

"So, Jamie, I don't think I've ever asked you what your major is," Lillian said in the middle of the meal.

"I'm going for teaching," said Jamie.

"Oh, what age?"

"Elementary," Jamie replied.

"Oh, that is so cute," Lillian said.

"Yeah, I love the kids at that age," said Jamie.

"I wish you could be my teacher," said Shane. "That'd really be cool."

"It would," Jamie frowned. "It's a shame I can't. By the time I get out of school and start teaching, you'll be out of elementary school."

"Dan, what are you going to do again?" Gabe asked.

"I don't really know," Daniel shrugged.

"I thought you had to choose a major," Ken said. "You did do that, right?"

"Well, yeah, while I was in Paris," said Daniel. "I just picked international relations because all of the credits from abroad would transfer. But I don't think there is anything I can actually do with that major. Maybe be a diplomat or something. I don't know."

"Why don't you think about law school?" Lillian asked.

"You always tell me to go to law school," said Daniel.

"I'm not telling you to go to law school," said Lillian. "I'm suggesting that you think about it. It's not a horrible idea."

"I just don't know what I want to do," Daniel shrugged. "But at least I don't have it as bad as Jake."

"Yeah, he is really stressing," Jamie agreed.

"About what?" Ken asked.

"He never seems stressed," said Gabe.

"He is," said Daniel. "He has always wanted to be a Marine, ever since we were kids."

"Being a Marine isn't a bad thing," Shane said. "Is it?"

"No, of course not," said Jamie. "We need the Marines. But Jake decided not to go, because of the swords, and because of Liz. Who is going to law school, by the way."

"I know, I know," Daniel laughed. "Maybe I'll go with her. We'll see. But anyway, Jake is really stressing about his decision. He just always needs to have a plan. I think his parents are kind of pressuring him, though he won't say. But not having a plan is killing him."

"He'll be OK," said Shane. "Right?"

"Of course he will," said Lillian. "Not having a plan might be scary, but he'll get through it. He needs to make the choice that is best for him."

"Yeah," said Daniel. "It just sucks that he has to make his choice right now."

"What do you mean, right now?" asked Gabe. "You guys don't graduate college for another two years."

"Yeah, but he would have to leave August first," said Daniel. "And then he wouldn't be coming back. So he literally needs to choose his life path in a few weeks."

"That's not true," said Ken. "He doesn't need to choose his life path now. He only needs to choose whether or not he wants to be a Marine. And I need to choose whether or not I want the last piece of steak. Which I do!"

The next morning Daniel was awakened by the feeling that someone was watching him. He opened his eyes to see Mercury hovering above his bed.

"WHOA!" Daniel shouted. "You know that's why people are scared of ghosts? They just kinda pop up! Don't do that!"

"You missed your training last night," Mercury said, ignoring him completely.

"What?" Daniel asked, still groggy. "Oh, yeah, I decided to have a nice night with my family and with Jamie."

"Instead of training?" Mercury asked. "That is unacceptable."

"Why?" Daniel asked. "We missed one night, it's not the end of the world."

"Are you sure about that?" Mercury asked.

"What?" Daniel asked.

"You must train hard to be as strong as you can be," Mercury said.

"We have been, and we will," said Daniel. "Besides, we beat the bad guys; don't we deserve a night off? We'll start training harder again when the boys get out of school."

"They could have come back," Mercury replied.

"The boys?" Daniel asked, still groggy.

"No!" Mercury said, a little too loud for Daniel. "Hellfire and Hornet!"

"And we would have beaten them again," said Daniel. "They couldn't have gotten stronger in one day, and we couldn't have gotten weaker by missing one day of training."

"Do not get cocky because of one victory," said Mercury. "And remember that you promised to protect the lives of others."

"At the expense of having a life for myself?" Daniel asked. "Like I said, one night could not have made a difference. They could not possibly have gotten stronger in one night."

"Oh, they couldn't have?" Mercury replied. "Are you sure?"

"What are you saying?" Daniel asked warily. "Is there something I should know?"

"Sorry, I do not wish to interfere in your life. Good-bye," said Mercury, and then he vanished.

"Stubborn sorcerer!" Daniel shouted after Mercury had disappeared, along with a few other choice terms. "Pretty soon the boys will be done with school, and then we can train in the morning, and actually have lives at night."

The next week went by quickly, and the younger boys found themselves done with school in a flash. Another year under their belts, they embraced the coming summer, which they knew would be an especially good one. They had their brothers back full time, they got to train with the Knights every day, and Jamie and Liz were around a lot. They were very fond of the two girls; in fact they liked those two better than any girls either of the older boys had ever dated. Ryan and Jeanne were also around a lot, and the younger boys enjoyed having them around.

The Saturday after school was out, all five boys were sitting in the Rubin house. It was only three o'clock, but they had already accomplished so much. Daniel's day had started at 7:30 a.m., when he went into the dojo to help teach the kids' classes. Shane came in at 9:30 for the advanced kids' class. The others had joined them at 10:30 for their own class, which Shane watched, and then they had all done their Knight training. They were trying to decide what to do for the rest of the day. They couldn't decide whether they wanted to go bowling, or to a movie, or any other of the many things there was to do on Long Island on a Saturday in the summer. Daniel and Jake decided to call the girls.

"Hello?" Liz answered the phone.

"Hey, it's Jake"

"Hey!" Liz replied.

"We were wondering if you ladies wanted to come out tonight," Jake said.

"Oh, sorry," Liz said. "We're having a girls' night out tonight with Jeanne."

"With Jeanne?" Jake asked.

"Yeah, we haven't really hung out with her since Paris," Liz answered. "We miss our Third Musketeer."

"Third Musketeer?" Jake asked. "I have never once heard you guys refer to yourselves as the Three Musketeers."

"Oh, I just made that up," Liz answered, laughing.

"Oh, OK, well then maybe Ryan is free," Jake said, half to himself.

"Maybe," said Liz. "Hey, why don't the six of us hang out tomorrow? We haven't done that in a while."

"OK, sounds good, call me when you wake up tomorrow," said Jake.

"Will you actually answer the phone?" Liz asked. "You have a bad habit of sleeping until two in the afternoon, and not answering the phone any earlier."

"Well, then, call Dan," said Jake. "He wakes up early."

"Eleven o'clock isn't that early, darling," Liz said.

"He wakes up earlier than that," Jake answered. "Whatever, just call somebody at some point, maybe we can go to the beach or something."

"Sounds like a plan," Liz answered, laughing. "Bye."

"Bye," said Jake, hanging up the phone.

"They're busy?" Daniel asked.

"Yeah, we're hanging out with them tomorrow," said Jake. "Oh, they said they're hanging out with Jeanne tonight, so why don't we call Ryan?"

"Cool," said Daniel. "And I know just the place to go."

"Lemme guess," said Jake. "The arcade."

"How'd you know?"

"You always wanna go to the arcade," Jake answered.

"Yeah, but so does everyone else," Daniel answered.

"No I agree," said Jake. "But still I knew what you were going to say."

"Congratulations, you must be picking it up from the sorcerer," Daniel replied. "You should take that act on the road."

Ryan met up with them, and they went to the giant arcade only a few minutes from their house. It always had all of the latest games, including a bowling alley and a laser tag room. It was certainly enough to keep them busy for a few hours.

The fighting games were their favorites, so they paired off and played against each other. Jake and Ryan were facing off, and right next to them Shane was trying to teach Daniel a lesson. That left Gabe and Robert together. They wandered around looking for an open game that they liked, but since it was the first Saturday of summer, most of the good games were taken. They decided to wait their turn on a game. The guy in front of them lost and moved out of the way, so they stepped up. Gabe had just put his money in when the guy came back.

"I was playing," the guy said.

"Oh, sorry," said Gabe. "I thought you were done."

"Well, I wasn't, and you stole my game," said the guy.

"OK, you can have this one, I'll play when you're finished," said Gabe.

"No way!" said Robert. "You can't take our game. You were totally done, you just wanna steal our money!"

"You calling me a liar?" the guy asked.

"No, he isn't," Gabe said. "You might be mistaken, however. It did look as though you were finished."

"I personally think you're a liar," said Robert. "Just a big, fat liar."

"Oh, really?" said the guy. "Hey, guys, this kid's calling me a liar!"

When he said this, three of his friends walked up. The four of them were all several inches taller than either Gabe or Robert, and much larger. They made a circle around Gabe and Robert, cracking their knuckles and smiling.

"Still think I'm a liar?" the first guy asked.

"Yeah, and you're ugly on top of it," said Robert. "And if you think you can intimidate us, that makes you stupid, too."

"Rob!" Gabe said to his friend. "Look, this is all just a big misunderstanding."

From across the room, Shane saw what was happening. "Hey, Dan, look," he said.

"Oh, boy," Daniel said, looking over. "Hey Jake, they're in trouble."

"Let's get a closer look, shall we?" Jake asked.

The four of them left their games and moved into the crowd that had formed around the spectacle.

"Let's help!" Shane said to Daniel.

"Six on four would be unfair," said Daniel. "Let's see how they handle it."

In the meantime, Gabe was trying to diffuse the situation. "Look, how about your next game is on me?" he asked,

"Tell your friend to apologize," said the guy.

"Fine," said Robert. "I'm sorry you're ugly."

"Rob, you aren't helping," said Gabe, doing a good job of hiding a chuckle.

"OK, OK," said Robert. "I'm sorry, it was all just a misunderstanding. Now let's get out of here."

"You're not forgiven!" said the guy.

He stepped in and threw a punch at Robert's face. Robert ducked out of the way, causing the guy to punch one of his large friends. As the two friends argued, Robert and Gabe snuck out of the circle.

"Time to go," said Daniel, coming up to them.

"Definitely," said Gabe, nodding.

As they stepped outside, Robert said, "Gabe, why'd you let that guy take your game?"

"It was only fifty cents," Gabe answered. "It just wasn't worth it to fight, and then we woulda gotten kicked out, or worse."

"We learned Ju-Jitsu so we can defend ourselves from guys like that," Robert said.

"No, we learned it so that we can if they leave us no choice," Jake said. "Not to start a fight, which is what you were doing. Even if you didn't throw the first punch you were still starting that fight with your attitude. And besides, before fighting we always try to talk our way out of it. We don't want to hurt people, even people that probably deserve it."

"I agree," said Ryan. "Fighting just isn't worth it."

"But we could have taken those guys no problem!" said Robert.

"Of course you could have," said Daniel. "We know you could have, and now they know you could have. Isn't that enough?"

"No," said Robert. "They don't know we could have."

"Maybe that's just as well," said Gabe. "They would have only learned the hard way. I only wish that I never have to make anyone learn the hard way how tough I am."

"And what if they attack us, and we don't have the opportunity to walk away like we just did?" Robert asked.

"Then it's time to do what you need to in order to defend yourself, or your loved ones," said Jake as they drove off.

The next day was a warm, sunny day at the end of June. Jamie and

Liz showed up at the Rubins' house just before lunchtime. Ryan and Jeanne were late, as usual. Daniel always said that Ryan was extremely dependable … tell him to show up at ten, and without fail, he would show up at eleven-thirty every time. So Jamie and Liz knocked on the door, knowing they would have time to get quite comfortable inside.

"Hey, girls," Lillian said as she opened the door. "They're around back finishing up their training. You can go around if you want."

"OK, thank you," both girls said, smiling.

Jamie and Liz walked into the backyard, and found the five boys lying on chairs on the deck with their eyes closed. The girls just assumed they were meditating, and didn't want to disturb them. Instead they decided to wait for them to finish.

"Hey Jamie, hey, Liz," Shane said as they walked onto the deck.

"I thought your eyes were supposed to be closed," Liz said.

"They are," Shane answered. "You two have very recognizable footsteps."

"Wow, you're getting good!" Jamie said.

"Well, what I'm wondering is why both of you are wearing long pants on such a hot day," said Robert. "I can tell because of the 'swoosh' noise they make as you walk."

"At least Jamie is wearing sandals," Gabe said. "Those flip-flops of yours make an interesting sound."

"Wow, you guys are getting really good!" Liz said. "Are you sure your eyes are closed?"

"Yes," all three answered at once.

"They are getting good," said Jake. "Of course the point of meditation is to block everything out and clear your mind totally, not to try to pay attention to things around you. But they're doing well anyway."

"Yeah, we're really proud of them," said Daniel.

"And me as well," said Mercury. "But that concludes our training session for today. Hopefully you won't hear from me until tomorrow."

With that, he disappeared. One by one, the five boys opened up their eyes and sat up. They all stayed sitting for a minute, then pushed themselves up. Gabe, Robert, and Shane ran off after saying their goodbyes; Daniel and Jake walked up to Jamie and Liz. They heard the doorbell ring, and knew that Ryan and Jeanne were there.

They ran through the house to meet their friends at the front door. They let them in, and, as usual, had to stop Roxy from jumping. She was getting better, but she was still just a little overzealous. Jeanne just walked straight into the kitchen, but Roxy caught Ryan. She jumped up on him, wagging her tail and trying to kiss him. She nearly knocked him back out of the front door before Daniel successfully pulled her off. Ryan quickly ran into the kitchen.

They all sat down to lunch, and after they had eaten Jeanne said, "So, I saw your story in the newspaper the other day."

"Which story?" Daniel asked.

"The one by the cop saying that you guys didn't kill those people," Jeanne answered.

"Oh, right," Daniel said. "That was really nice of him. We have to remember to send a gift basket to Sergeant Michaels at some point."

"A gift basket?" Jake asked.

"Yeah, to thank him," Daniel answered.

"Just put him on your holiday card list," Ryan said, smiling.

"So who were those other two guys?" Jeanne asked.

"They called themselves Hellfire and Hornet," Daniel said.

"But who were they, and what did they have to do with you?" asked Jamie.

"Well, as it turns out there are really four swords, not two," Jake answered. "They hold the other two."

"But I thought you have to help people with the swords," Liz said. "Or else you can't use them. Are those swords evil?"

"No, it is up to the holder to choose a path," said Daniel. "The swords are both good and evil, or so Mercury says."

"So they chose to get themselves rich?" Ryan asked.

"I guess so," Jake said, shrugging.

"But they didn't count on having to do battle with the Knights!" Ryan added.

"Actually, I think they did," said Daniel. "I think they were planning on us trying to stop them. In fact, I think they wanted it, so they could get us out of the way quick. They just didn't count on us being stronger than them."

"I got that feeling, too," said Jake. "I mean, they offered us a chance to join them, but I think they just wanted us to let our guard down."

"Think they'll be back?" Ryan asked.

"Oh, I'm counting on it," said Daniel. "In fact, I look forward to it."

"They'll have us right there to knock them down again," said Jake.

"Damn straight," said Daniel. "But enough about them. I need a short break from Knighthood. Let's go for a swim."

They all quickly got their bathing suits on and dove into the pool. The cool water was a good contrast to the hot, muggy day, especially for Daniel and Jake, who were still a little sweaty from their training. They generally liked to shower off before seeing the girls, and definitely preferred to smell nice, but it did not seem to be an option that day.

While they were in the pool, Daniel said, "Oh, yeah, I almost forgot. We're having a big Fourth of July party here. Jake's whole family is coming, and pretty much all of my relatives. My mom said I could invite you guys."

"That sounds cool; when is that?" Ryan asked.

"Well, we generally have Fourth of July parties on the Fourth of July," said Daniel, smiling.

"Oh, then, sorry, I can't," said Ryan. "I have plans with my family."

"Jeanne?" Jake asked.

"Well, Ryan invited me with him," Jeanne answered.

"Oh, OK," said Daniel. "Girls?"

"Sorry, got plans with my family," Jamie said.

"Me, too, sorry," Liz said.

"Fine," said Jake. "We don't need you guys anyway. We can have fun just us."

"We always do," said Daniel. "Besides we'll have Gabe, Robbie, and Shane. It'll still be a lot of fun."

Mercury opened his eyes after watching the scene in his mind. Daniel was definitely his favorite. He liked Jake, but there was just something special about Daniel. Daniel reminded him of himself when he was younger … much younger, of course. Daniel was complex, and yet so simple at the same time. He had a good heart, and was perhaps just a little naïve. Daniel let so few people near him, but those he did he trusted with his very life. He would never suspect one of those people of revealing his weaknesses to his enemy. Mercury hated being the one that Daniel shouldn't have trusted, but the safety of the world was more important than one life, however unfortunate that fact may seem.

"Are you sure they will both be at this address on July fourth?" Hellfire asked.

"Certain," the sorcerer replied.

Chapter 7

The Return

On the Fourth of July, Daniel woke up in a somewhat peculiar way. It was not as bad as the time that Mercury had woken him, but it was peculiar nonetheless. He remotely heard Shane's voice in his dreams, though he could not quite make out what his brother was saying. Then, suddenly, he felt something licking his face.

"Shane!" he yelled. "Stop licking me!"

"It's not me," Shane replied, laughing at him. "It's Roxy."

Daniel opened his eyes. "Oh, so it is," he said. "Good morning, girl."

"Mom says you have to come down and help," Shane said.

"What time is it?" Daniel asked.

"Almost ten, which gives us a little over an hour," Shane answered.

"Oh, wow," Daniel said, sitting up. "I'll be right down."

Daniel quickly put on a pair of shorts, threw in his contacts, brushed his teeth, and went downstairs. He saw that there was still quite a bit to do. He had always hated cleaning, but he figured that since he had vowed to help out the world, that included helping his parents whenever he could as well. If anyone had asked him, he would say that he preferred doing battle with vicious gunmen to housework. But he did it anyway. It would be mostly an outdoor party, so the deck needed to be cleaned. It was a warm day, and people would want to swim, so the pool needed to be cleaned as well. People would be inside also, so the house needed to be cleaned. And all of this was not even including the food, which Ken was taking care of.

It was Daniel's job to clean the pool, which he didn't mind too much. It was much better than vacuuming, which was Shane's job. Gabe was cleaning the deck, making sure that people would be able to sit and eat comfortably. Shane finished the vacuuming quickly and went out to help Ken with the food, one of his favorite activities. Daniel also finished his task quickly as the pool was not very dirty, and then he helped Gabe finish up the deck. Then they went inside to watch TV until the Raines family came.

When they did, they all went out onto the back porch. Ed joined Ken at the barbecue, while Gabe, Shane, and Robert went right into the pool. Daniel sat with Jake, Marie, and his mother to talk until lunch was ready.

"So, Dan, how are things?" Marie asked. "Jake and Robbie always come over here, I feel like I never see you."

"Things are going well," Daniel replied. "We're training really hard, so that takes up a lot of time. And we spend a lot of time with Jamie and Liz, and Ryan and Jeanne, too. So it's a busy but fun summer."

"Don't forget saving the world and whatnot," Lillian smiled.

"I don't know about the whole world," Daniel shrugged. "But I guess we've done some good."

"Certainly," Marie nodded. "Have you thought about what you are going to do after college?"

"A lot of people have asked me that," said Daniel. "But I'm only a sophomore, I've got two years left."

"You're not a sophomore anymore," Marie corrected.

"Although he does have two years left," said Lillian. "Plenty of time to figure it out. No rush."

"Jake doesn't have a plan either," said Marie.

"He's going to get one soon, though," said Ed, walking over and putting his hands on Jake's shoulders. "Isn't that right, Jacob?"

"Of course, Dad," Jake replied. "You know I've been really busy."

"I know," said Ed. "But how long are you going to use that as an excuse? You have to find something soon."

"I'll find something," Jake replied, adjusting so that his father's hands fell from his shoulders. "I'll find something really soon."

Nobody really knew what to say after that. The silence was growing a little uncomfortable when Gabe walked up with Robert and Shane.

"Anybody wanna go swimming?" Gabe asked.

"I'd love to; it's hot out here!" said Daniel.

"Sure, sounds good," said Jake.

They quickly got their bathing suits on, and soon there was a line at the diving board. Daniel went first, doing his usual back flip for his first dive. Jake did the same right after him. Gabe followed with a one-and-a-half front flip, his favorite dive. Robert followed doing a regular front flip, with Shane doing the same right after him. They kept doing dives, showing off and challenging one another. At one point Robert did a back dive, but pushed off of the board too hard, and his feet came around and landed with a huge splash.

"Man, that was ugly," Gabe said.

"You got a problem with my dives?" Robert asked.

"Not at all," said Gabe. "That was just the worst back dive I've ever seen."

"Well, then show me how it's done, oh, Dive Master," Robert mocked.

"Fine," Gabe said, getting out of the water defiantly. He walked to the end of the diving board, turned around, and shouted, "Now this is how you do a back dive!"

With that he launched himself off the board. He kept his body completely straight, as he should have. He kept his hands above his head, as he should have. He made one major mistake, however. He under-rotated, and when he hit the water, he was flat on his back. He entered with a loud *smack!* The others could almost hear his screams from underneath the water.

"Ohhhh, so that's how it's done!" Robert said, laughing hysterically, as Gabe surfaced.

"Yes, yes it is," said Gabe, just floating. "Now I wanna see you do it just like that."

"Sorry, I missed the entry," Robert said, still laughing. "Can you demonstrate it again?"

"Sure, just lemme regrow the skin on my back, OK?"

"Yeah, that looked painful," Daniel said. "You all right?"

"I'm fine, I just need to float for a minute."

The others kept doing dives and playing games. Gabe eventually recovered and rejoined the others in their horseplay. He didn't dive anymore for a while, but he did wrestle with them, joined in their chicken fights, and was involved in the epic Great Noodle Battle. They were in the pool almost the whole day. They got out for lunch, waited their mandatory half hour or so, and then went straight back in. They were in the pool long after the party ended, all of the guests had left, and their parents had gone down to the basement to watch television. Suddenly, Daniel noticed a strange shadow.

It was a slightly cloudy day, so the others did not seem to notice. The shadow gave Daniel a feeling in the pit of his stomach that he did not like. He looked around frantically, trying to find the cause. It was expanding, getting larger and lighter. Finally, he found the cause, and it made his heart pound in his chest. The others saw the shadow just as he had found the cause.

"What is that?" Shane asked.

"I don't know," said Gabe.

"Do you guys know?" Robert asked Daniel and Jake.

"Get inside, now!" Daniel shouted suddenly.

"Why?" asked Shane.

"Just do it!" Daniel shouted again. The three boys reluctantly ran into the house, not even stopping to dry off.

"It's Hellfire," said Jake.

"I was going to say the same thing," said Daniel. "But where is Hornet?"

Jake didn't have time to answer. Hellfire suddenly shot down, straight for the pool. As he got closer, it became clear that he was headed straight for Daniel. He took out his sword as he rapidly approached. Daniel ducked under the water just as Hellfire flew over, slashing down at him. Blood rose into the water, and Daniel popped back up in the middle of it.

"Dan!" Jake cried.

"It's OK, he just got me in the shoulder," said Daniel.

"Thank God you're OK," Jake said. "But we have to get out of the pool, we're sitting ducks in here."

Jake quickly got out. It took Daniel a little longer, because he could only use his right arm, which was luckily his stronger one. While he was on the ladder dragging himself out, Hellfire made his second pass. He headed straight for Daniel once again, sword drawn. Before he got to Daniel, however, he was hit by a rock. He wasn't hurt, merely annoyed, but he wheeled around to look at Jake, who had thrown it.

"Come on, right here!" yelled Jake, trying to give Daniel some time to get onto dry land.

Hellfire shot at Jake with rage in his eyes. He swung for Jake's chest, but Jake had fast enough reflexes to jump out of the way. Hellfire's slash missed its intended target, but instead sliced deep into Jake's right leg. A large cut opened on Jake's thigh as he dove out of the way. Jake was flat on the ground, and Hellfire stood above him. He was about to finish Jake off when Daniel came running up. He dove at Hellfire, who merely swatted him away. It gave Jake just enough time to get back to his feet.

"Dan, you OK?" Jake asked, limping over to his friend.

"I'm fine, you?" Daniel asked, using his right arm to push himself up.

"Just peachy," said Jake.

Hellfire slowly approached them, still on his shield.

"Hey, ugly!" Robert yelled. Hellfire turned to him. "Yeah, you!" Robert continued.

"Rob, no!" Jake yelled.

"But we can help!" Gabe replied.

"Get back inside and stay there!" Jake yelled back.

"Let us help!" Shane cried.

"Do as Jake says," Daniel replied. "That'll be helping us!"

"Just so you know, it won't matter where they are," said Hellfire. "After I finish you two, they will be my first victims."

He sped toward the Knights again. This time they both dove out of the way, unharmed.

Mercury! Daniel thought. *We could really use the swords right about now!*

"They're on their way," Mercury replied. "Just hold on a bit longer."

It had better be quick, Jake thought.

Hellfire came toward Daniel again. Jake, ignoring the pain as much as he could, ran and leapt at Hellfire. Hellfire swatted him away, and still moved forward at Daniel. Daniel dove under the sword just as it sped toward him, and a small cut opened up on his back. He came up and kicked at Hellfire, who caught the foot. He spun Daniel around by his foot and threw him at Jake, who was just getting up. They crashed to the ground together.

"This isn't working," Jake said, forcing himself up without putting weight on his right leg.

"Tell me about it," Daniel said, his left arm hanging completely limp at his side.

They looked up to see Hellfire floating slowly toward them on his shield. They stumbled backwards, not having much of anywhere else to go. Both were feeling weary from blood loss. Still he slowly came toward them, and they could tell he enjoyed torturing them. They backed until they felt a wall behind them. It was the fence at the side of the yard, there was nowhere else for them to go. Suddenly, the two swords fell from the sky and stuck into the ground right in front of them. They looked up and saw their shields flying overhead. They couldn't help but smile as they straightened up. Hellfire stopped advancing. The boys looked at each other, nodded, and grabbed their swords.

They felt the power run through them as they transformed into the Knights. The injured limbs were still immobile, but the armor had temporarily stopped the bleeding. Both were still somewhat dizzy from blood loss, but the power of the swords gave them extra energy. Jake could limp, though he could not walk or run, and it seemed as though kicking was out of the question. Daniel's left arm was immobile, which made it a good thing that he was right-handed.

"This oughta even things out," Daniel said.

"I don't know about that," Hellfire said. "But it should definitely make things a little more interesting."

Daniel and Jake moved forward and slashed simultaneously at Hellfire. He easily stopped their attack. They tried to push him back by putting pressure on the swords, but they could not. He simply lifted his arm, throwing their hands into the air, and then, with one movement, he kicked them both. They both went flying back.

"He's stronger than both of us put together!" Jake said.

"How is that possible?" Daniel asked.

"Wait, look at his sword!" Jake said. "He's got two gems on each side!"

Daniel looked, and saw that Jake was correct. Hellfire's sword had both a red and an orange gem on both sides. Hellfire had not changed in appearance, however, which is why they hadn't noticed before.

"But how is that possible? And what does it mean?" Daniel asked.

For the second time that day, Daniel got no answer. Hellfire sped toward him, jumping off his shield this time. Both of his feet crashed into Daniel's chest, sending Daniel slamming to the ground with Hellfire on top of him. He began to repeatedly kick Daniel in the face, raising his sword.

Jake, ignoring the pain, ran up and leapt at Hellfire, who caught him by the throat in midair. Jake kicked as Hellfire tightened his grip. Hellfire called his shield to him and, still holding onto Jake, rose high into the air. He then sped down and released Jake, sending him crashing into the ground. Both Knights were down.

Hellfire laughed. "This is even easier than I thought it would be."

He moved slowly toward Daniel first. He wanted to savor every moment of his victory. After he killed these two, there would be nothing to stop him. He would have ultimate power. He hovered above Daniel, absorbing the last few drops of joy out of the situation. Then he raised his sword without noticing the back door opening and three boys running out into the yard.

Shane leapt off the deck, landing on Hellfire's back, putting his hands around the villain's neck. He held as tightly as he could while Hellfire began to shake him around. He had held on for only a little while when Hellfire grabbed him by the hands and threw him onto the ground. Hellfire raised his sword, looking at his attacker. Then he lowered the sword.

"No, I don't think I will kill you now," Hellfire said. "I have to deal with the Knights first. Besides, what could someone so small possibly do to stop me?"

Shane stumbled away as two new attackers leapt from the deck. Hellfire was caught unaware again, and Gabe and Robert landed their hardest kicks to his back. The double strike did little more than knock Hellfire forward a bit. He turned around and hit them both, sending them flying back. When he turned around, the Knights were back on their feet.

"Your brothers are very brave, but they cannot hurt me!" Hellfire said to them, laughing as they struggled to stay conscious.

"Maybe they weren't trying to hurt you," Daniel said. "Maybe they were just giving us time to get up."

"And as long as we're up, we have a chance," said Jake.

"You have no chance!" Hellfire shouted. "Getting up just prolongs your torture!"

He flew forward, at Jake first this time. Jake attempted to throw a punch as he came in, but it was blocked. Hellfire's fist went crashing into Jake's stomach, sending the hero collapsing to his knees. Hellfire was about to finish Jake when Daniel ran up, and met Hellfire's fist with his face. He stumbled back, then Hellfire came at him again. This time when he punched Daniel it sent the Knight clear across the pool. Hellfire jumped onto his shield and headed straight across the pool at Daniel, crossing the paths where Gabe was laying.

"Gabe, catch!" yelled Shane, tossing Gabe the metal pool skewer.

Hellfire, having forgotten about the others, flew low so he could finish Daniel off as quickly as possible. As he flew by, Gabe swung the skewer as hard as he could into Hellfire's ankles. Hellfire wasn't ready for this, and went tumbling off his shield into the pool.

"Nice!" Robert yelled.

Within seconds, however, there came a huge splash as Hellfire jumped out of the pool, twenty feet into the air. He was going to come down straight at Gabe. Daniel jumped from the other side of the pool. Hellfire's back was turned, so Daniel got a clear kick in, sending Hellfire spiraling straight down toward Jake, who was now back on his feet. Jake threw a punch as hard as he could into Hellfire's face as he fell.

Hellfire got up slowly, having been injured by that last attack. Still, though, the Knights were more injured than he was, and he was far more powerful.

"Let's make this more interesting, shall we?" Hellfire said.

Just then the red shield swooped down. Hellfire jumped on, and shot off into the distance.

"We've got to follow him!" Jake said.

"That's what he wants us to do," Daniel said.

"But if we don't he'll just come back and attack us again," Jake replied. "Besides, he's injured right now; we may never get another chance like this!"

"All right," Daniel said. "Gabe, Rob, Shane, go inside; we'll be back in a little while."

"Hopefully," Jake added so softly that only Daniel could hear.

Their shields picked them up and they were on their enemy's trail. He was injured, but he could still push his shield to full speed. Luckily, having four gems on his sword did not make his shield faster, and they could stay close to him. Daniel's arm was throbbing; it felt like it might fall off any second, but he didn't have it as bad as Jake. Jake's leg was on fire as he bent his knees to ride the shield. He dealt with the pain the only way he knew how: by turning it into anger and using it.

They were having a hard time controlling the shields at full speed with their injuries. They slowed down only a little bit, enough to keep control over the shields, yet still going fast enough to keep the red shield in sight. They were out over the water now; they recognized the area well. They were nearing the bridge on the Robert Moses Causeway that led to the beach. They saw the red shield descend onto the bridge, and followed.

There were two bridges out to the Robert Moses beaches. Generally they carried traffic two different ways. But recently there had been construction on one of the bridges, so all the traffic was backed up across the one two-lane bridge. They found the red shield on the bridge that was under construction. They were surprised to find no Hellfire, however. They looked all around, even at the workers who were looking very confused, but there was no sign of Hellfire. They jumped off their shields to get ready to fight. They were positive that Hellfire was planning to spring a trap.

They walked around the bridge, half noticing the unfinished construction. Suddenly, Daniel thought he heard something above him. Instinctively he rolled out of the way just as Hellfire came crashing down onto the bridge, exactly where Daniel had been standing. When the smoke cleared, they saw Hellfire standing on the bridge in front of them. When they looked closer, they noticed that Hellfire had actually put his foot clear through the unfinished bridge.

"Glad I rolled," Daniel said.

"Yeah, you're not kidding," Jake agreed.

They soon realized that Hellfire was not saying anything. He seemed to be struggling. Then it hit them: he had put his foot through the bridge, but could not get it out. He began to thrash about, pulling as hard as he could. His powerful legs were enough to shake the bridge, but not to release his foot from the concrete block in which it was stuck. He began to squirm more violently, and the bridge began to crumble around him.

"Stop!" Jake cried. "You'll bring the whole bridge down!"

"Let us help you!" Daniel shouted.

"Leave me alone!" Hellfire shouted back.

The harder he pulled, the more the bridge crumbled. It was falling apart under the stress of his mighty struggle, but still his foot did not come free. The bridge finally began to crack around him. He was going to fall into the water, with his foot trapped in the giant block of cement.

"This is nuts!" Jake said.

"Yeah, we gotta do something!" Daniel answered.

"OK, you get Hellfire, and I'll get the workmen out!" Jake said.

"All right!"

The shields came down and picked them up. Jake grabbed the nearby workmen and flew them to safety on the other bridge, where traffic had stopped completely to watch the struggle. The workers were scared and confused, but they thanked him heartily. He made sure that there were no other workers on the bridge, and turned to watch Daniel and Hellfire.

The bridge under Hellfire had given way shortly after they had gotten on the shields. The rest of the bridge would soon follow, but Daniel was only worried about Hellfire. He was falling toward the water, still attached to a piece of mixed cement and steel larger than a truck.

Daniel sped toward him, trying to figure out how to free the trapped villain. As he came closer, however, Hellfire slashed at him. The strike did not come close to hitting Daniel, but rather had quite a different effect from the one intended. The swing was powerful enough to flip the piece of bridge over, so that Hellfire was underneath it. He hit the water with two tons of solid concrete mixed with steel on top of him. They waited for him to rise, but he did not.

Chapter 8

Life Goes On

Very slowly, Daniel and Jake made their way home. They were bruised, battered, and bleeding, and felt no need to push themselves too hard. Neither of them said a word on the way back; both were too busy concentrating on staying conscious. Their adrenaline had kept them awake through the fight, but now it was leaving them. When they reached home, their shields departed, and their parents rushed them straight to the hospital.

They climbed into the ambulance, and then everything went black for both of them. They woke up to voices, though they still could not see anything.

"They lost a lot of blood; it's amazing they're still alive," said a voice. "Had you gotten them to us only a half hour later, we might not have been able to save them."

"We got them here as soon as we could," Daniel heard his mother reply.

He squinted open his eyes to see her talking to a doctor in the hall. He looked around, and saw that he was being given blood and painkillers through an IV, and his heart rate was being monitored. Jake was getting the same treatment. Jake opened his eyes only a few minutes later, after Daniel's mother closed the door to the hall to give them some rest.

"You know you saved my life back there, more than once," Daniel said, when he was sure Jake was awake. "Thanks."

"Don't mention it," Jake replied. "Besides, you saved me a few times, too."

"I'm just glad you're in this with me," Daniel said.

"Same here," said Jake. "We'll always be there for each other."

"Good, 'cause I couldn't do it alone," Daniel replied, a lump catching in his throat.

"Good, cause I wouldn't let you," Jake said with a smile.

Just then, Gabe, Robert, and Shane walked into the room. "You guys OK?" Gabe asked.

"I've been better," Daniel said.

"Yeah, me, too," said Jake. "But it sure beats being dead."

"I'm glad you guys made it," said Shane.

"You had us worried for a while," said Robert.

"We wouldn't have made it without you guys," Daniel said.

"He's right," Jake agreed. "You showed real courage standing up to Hellfire like that."

"We couldn't stand by and watch you get hurt," said Gabe. "That's why we've been training so hard with you guys. Just in case you needed us."

It was then that the doctor walked in. "So how exactly did this happen?" he asked.

"Lawnmower accident," said Daniel.

"Ouch," the doctor said. "Well, it looks like you two were extremely lucky."

"Lucky?" Jake asked incredulously. "You call this lucky?"

"Well, for one thing, Mr. Raines, one inch more to the inside of your thigh and you would have sliced a major vein. The saphenous vein, to be more specific. The bleeding would be almost uncontrollable. Then you'd be dead for sure. One inch down and you would have severed the tendons in the knee, making it so that you could never walk properly again." Turning to Daniel, the doctor continued, "Mr. Rubin, one inch higher and you would have sliced the carotid artery, the artery that brings blood up to your brain. You would have been dead almost instantly. And you should regain full mobility of your arm. And both of you have only minor injuries other than that. In fact, I say that you will both be back to fighting strength in a little over a month."

"I don't think we'll be doing any fighting for a while," Daniel said.

"It's just an expression," the doctor replied. "I'll leave you alone now for a while; you have visitors."

"So it's Daniel Rubin and Jacob Raines, is it?" Sergeant John Michaels asked as he walked in.

"How did you … ?" Jake asked, trying to sit up.

"Don't worry, I won't tell," said Sergeant Michaels. "I heard about the fight on the bridge, then checked hospitals for blade wounds to the leg or shoulders."

"How did you know to check for that?" Daniel asked. "We received the wounds before we wound up on the bridge."

"Yes, but from witness accounts, the Green Knight had no use of his left arm, meaning a wound to the shoulder or upper arm, and the Blue Knight had no use of his right leg, meaning a wound to the thigh or hip." Sergeant Michaels replied. "And I figured the only ones that could wound you guys would be the other two, so I knew they had to be blade wounds."

"Very good," said Jake. "But now what?"

"I'm just here to give you these," the Sergeant said, setting down two bouquets of flowers. "And to say thanks for surviving … the world still needs your help. Now get some rest."

"He's really a nice guy," Jake said after Sergeant Michaels had left.

"He was really worried about both of you," Liz added as she and Jamie walked in.

"We were all worried about you," Jamie agreed.

"Sorry, we didn't mean to worry you," Daniel said. "We didn't exactly plan for this to happen."

"Well, I should hope not!" Jamie said with a laugh as she sat down at the foot of Daniel's bed.

"You didn't have to come down to see us," Daniel said to her, the smile fading from his face.

"I know," Jamie answered. "But what kind of girlfriend would I be if I didn't come down here?"

"Not a very good one, I guess," Daniel agreed.

"Well I'm glad you guys are here," Jake said.

"Wouldn't miss it for the world," Liz said. "Besides, I hear they're gonna have a great fireworks special here later on tonight."

"Are we still gonna be here tonight?" Daniel asked. "What time are we leaving?"

"We hear you guys are spending the night," Liz said.

"I'm kinda jealous," Jamie said. "You guys get to get waited on hand and foot."

"There are worse things, I guess," Jake said.

"Well, look who's awake!" Lillian Rubin said as she walked in the room.

"Finally," Marie Raines said, behind her.

"You guys gave us quite a scare!" Ken Rubin added.

"Tell me about it; that's not how we want to find out that you saved the world!" Ed Raines said walking in with him.

"We're glad you're safe now," said Lillian.

"It's over now," Daniel said.

"That's right, no more Hellfire," Jake agreed.

"We're glad it is," Marie said, kissing her son on the forehead. "But now we're all going to leave, because you need your rest."

Daniel and Jake said good-bye as their friends and family left them alone in their hospital room. It was true that they could have been in a worse situation: They both had personal televisions and personal nurses. They could wheel their IVs into the bathroom should they need to go, but mostly they could just sit in bed and do nothing. Neither of them had any trouble sleeping that night, after everything they had gone through. It was the first Fourth of July they could remember that they didn't see fireworks, though they had seen stars.

For the next few days they did very little. They both hated being injured, but neither could deny that they needed at least a few days' rest.

Apart from their major wounds, their other bumps and bruises had not yet healed, so they took it easy like the doctor said. They watched television, read books, played video games, and sat by the pool. In all honesty they didn't mind taking a few days off from being the Knights, especially after that last battle. THE last battle.

The other three boys, however, took no time off. They trained harder than ever, even without their older brothers there. They had seen firsthand how powerful enemies could be, and knew they could not afford to slack off at all. And even though Hellfire was dead, they figured they might be needed sometime in the future. With their brothers temporarily out of commission, they might need to step in. They hoped that their battle was not over, but just beginning.

Less than a week after the battle, Daniel and Jake walked out of a movie theater along with Gabe, Shane, Robert, Jamie, Liz, Ryan, and Jeanne. They walked slowly in order to keep pace with Jake, who was pushing himself along with his cane. Daniel adjusted the strap pinning his left arm in its sling to his chest, keeping the arm immobile.

"So what did everyone think of the movie?" Liz asked.

"I thought it was awesome," said Jake.

"Yeah, me, too," said Robert. "I love superhero movies. And now it reminds me of you guys."

"Except you guys are cooler," said Gabe, "because you're real."

"Yeah, and we get to train with you," said Shane.

"I thought the special effects were awesome," said Jeanne. "It's amazing what they can do these days."

"Yeah, the fight scenes were incredible," Ryan nodded. "Although I bet it was nowhere near as real as when you guys do it!"

"Well, duh," Jake laughed. "I mean, we do have guns shoved into our chests and swords flying at our faces. It doesn't get more real than that. But this movie was great."

"I'm a little surprised that you liked it," said Liz.

"Why?" asked Jake. "I mean, what's not to love? He's got super powers, he always saves the day, and he gets the girl at the end. Plus, some bad guy butt-whooping."

"That's my favorite part," Shane smiled wide. "Like when you guys were beating Hellfire all over the backyard."

"He got us pretty good, too," Jake smiled.

The conversation continued, but Daniel was not a part of it. He was walking slightly ahead of everyone else, deep in thought.

"What's the matter?" Jamie whispered, taking his hand. "Does your arm hurt?"

"No, it's nothing," Daniel shrugged.

"Oh, come on," Jamie said, smiling. "I know you too well for that. Now, what's wrong?"

"I don't know," Daniel shrugged again. "It's just, that movie."

"It was about a superhero," said Jamie. "I thought you'd love it. Right up your alley."

"I did," Daniel replied. "But, I mean that guy could do everything. He was so strong, so fast, everything."

"Well, yeah, thus the 'super' part," Jamie said, laughing.

"It's not that," said Daniel. "I mean, even when the chips were down, and when nothing was going his way, he still fought his heart out. He put his life on the line to save the world, even though it looked like he wasn't going to survive."

"But he did survive," Jamie said, looking into his eyes. "Besides, it's just a movie."

"No, it isn't," said Daniel. "Not for me. I mean, what if I have to make that choice some day? I don't know if I could put my life on the line to save the world. I'm only a superhero because I have the sword."

"That's not true," Jamie replied. "When Hellfire was attacking you the other day, what were you thinking?"

"I wasn't thinking about saving the world, if that's what you're asking," Daniel responded.

"What were you thinking?" Jamie asked.

"I was thinking about saving my own butt," said Daniel. "Just making sure that I got out of there alive."

"Why didn't you run away then?" Jamie asked.

Daniel shrugged. "Because then he would have hurt my family and my friends."

"Well, there you go," said Jamie. "It doesn't have to be about saving the whole world. Maybe it is just about saving the people that you love."

"But the guy in the movie thought about saving the world," said Daniel.

"That was a movie." Jamie smiled. "You're a real person. Nobody is writing a script about what you should be thinking about. You are flesh and blood, and you have a real mind and a real heart. What is it you always tell me about true power? Does true power really come from swords, or guns, or muscles?"

"True power comes from the heart," Daniel replied.

"Exactly," said Jamie. "You said it yourself. Look, the way I see it is this: You are a superhero. Get that? A super-hero. The sword is what makes you super, that's true. Although I think you're pretty super," she said, taking hold of his uninjured arm.

"Funny," Daniel chuckled.

"But anyway," Jamie continued. "Sure, the sword is what makes you super. But YOU are what makes you a hero. Look at Hellfire. He sure is super, but is he a hero?"

"No way," Daniel shook his head. "Not by my definition."

"Not by anyone's definition," Jamie agreed. "Maybe without the sword you wouldn't be a SUPERhero, but you would absolutely still be a hero. You were fighting to protect the people that you care about. I know you, you have a huge heart. You care about so many people, and so many people care about you. And if you fight with your heart, and fight to protect those people that you care about, then there is NOTHING that you can't do."

"Thanks." Daniel smiled, and leaned in to give her a quick kiss.

"Now let's wait for the others," Jamie said, smiling back.

Exactly ten days from their initial hospitalization, Daniel and Jake returned to the hospital to have their stitches removed and their wounds inspected. The doctor was impressed at how well they were doing. After removing the stitches he told them that they could go back to business as usual, though no strenuous physical activity. Obviously, they thought, he did not understand their business as usual.

"Finally," Daniel said as they left. "I've been dying of boredom."

"Hey, at least you could walk around," Jake said. "If I wanted to take a walk I woulda had to walk on my hands."

"They gave you a cane!" Daniel said. "And at least you could cut your own food; my mommy had to cut all mine."

They both went back to Daniel's house. Everyone had been dying to see them after they saw the doctor, looking to share the moment with them. Daniel and Jake were waiting on their friends when Mercury appeared.

"Good to see you two healthy again," Mercury said.

"It's good to *be* healthy again," Daniel said.

"When can you guys start training?" Mercury asked.

"Not for a few weeks still," Jake said. "Doctor wants us to rest for a while."

"Very well," Mercury said. "Oh, by the way, have you seen your brothers lately?"

"Yeah, we see them every day," said Daniel.

"No, I meant have you seen them train?" Mercury said.

"Oh, no," Daniel answered. "Why?"

"They are doing very well," Mercury replied. "Gabe and Robert might catch up to you guys soon if you don't start training again."

"Wow, that's awesome," Jake said. "What about Shane?"

"He is trying very hard," said Mercury. "He is not quite at their level, and not as strong as an adult yet, but I should think that you would not find even a preteen or teenager that is stronger than he. And he definitely has the same fire that the rest of you have."

"Fire?" asked Jake. "What do you mean?"

"The warrior quality," Mercury answered. "The mentality that you will never give up, to fight until you drop, to constantly improve. He definitely has that fire."

"Yeah, I'll agree with that," Daniel said. "You should be around when my parents tell him it's bedtime. Stand clear when that happens."

"You know it's a shame they can't have swords, too," Jake said.

"They will make excellent heroes when their time comes," Mercury said, and then vanished abruptly.

"Did he say *will?*" Daniel asked.

"Don't read too much into it," Jake said.

"But I thought there were only four swords," Daniel said. "So either there is one we don't know about, or one of us is going to die?"

"Don't talk like that," Jake said. "Hellfire is dead, and the other two swords were lost."

"Right, but we don't know what happened to Hornet, and, like you said, we never recovered the sword," Daniel said. "I have the feeling that this adventure is not over yet."

"Can we make dinner before solving the mystery?" Jake asked. "Liz and them are going to be here in a little over an hour; maybe we should get ready."

"Sure," Daniel shrugged. "I can't help wondering, though."

The next few weeks went by very quickly for Daniel and Jake. Each day they were able to do more and more, easing their way back into their training. They found that after two more weeks they were just about fully back into their normal routine. Their sensei asked Daniel to teach kids' classes six days a week, and he trained with Jake in adult classes four days a week. They had been absent from the dojo for over a month, and it felt good to be back. They felt the same way after this short absence as they had after being in Paris. Ju-Jitsu was their hobby, but the dojo was a part of their lives.

While Daniel and Jake were concentrating on their recovery, the younger boys had to start worrying about school again. The summer months went by too fast as it was, but now they had to start worrying about school in late July. Apart from summer assignments, school sports were starting up again. Gabe was doing soccer and Robert was doing football, both of which demanded a good deal of their time. And there was a welcome day for incoming freshmen at the high school. Gabe and Robert were on the student council, so they had to go help. Shane, not having anything better to do, went with them.

When they got to the high school, Gabe and Robert went to check in. They learned that it would be their jobs to direct traffic in the halls. They soon found that the job held far less excitement than it promised, especially since most incoming freshmen and their parents were on guided tours. Shane was particularly bored, and quickly remembered that he did not actually have to be there, so he went walking around on his own.

"But don't go too far," Gabe said to him as he walked away.

"Don't worry, *Mom*, I won't," Shane called back.

He wandered around, not really having anywhere to go. Everything seemed so big to him, coming from the elementary school. The lockers were twice his size, and he wondered how anyone could use them. He kept walking around until he saw something interesting—an old picture from about four years earlier, of the varsity tennis team. And there, in the line, was Daniel. He looked at the old picture of his brother, trying to imagine what Daniel had been thinking at the time of the picture. Judging by the scowl on his face, he had probably been thinking, *If I had known it was picture day, I would have done my hair a bit better.* He was laughing at his brother when he heard footsteps behind him.

"You lost, punk?" said a voice.

Shane turned around. When he saw his old nemesis Melvin, he groaned. The bully had even acquired a new, and bigger, friend.

"Well?" Melvin snarled. "I asked you a question."

"No, I'm not lost," said Shane.

"Then what are you doing here?" the bully demanded. "You're not going into high school."

"So? Neither are you!" Shane retorted.

"My brother is," the kid replied, indicating the larger boy with him. "Anyway, what are you doing here?"

"I'm kinda just walking around," Shane said with a shrug.

"Well, you're walking down the wrong hall," Melvin responded sharply. "You know you got my mom fired."

"So this is the punk that got Mom fired?" said the bully's brother.

"Sorry," Shane said quickly.

"Don't say that; you aren't sorry!" Melvin answered.

"You know, you're right," said Shane. "I'm not sorry! She was a horrible principal, and she deserved to be fired."

"You better take that back!" said the older brother, advancing toward Shane.

"I told you, I can't," Shane shrugged. "It's the truth."

The two kept advancing on Shane until he found the wall behind him. He wasn't afraid of Melvin, but the older brother was almost twice his size. There was no way that he could end the fight without hurting the other boys. It looked as though Shane had no choice but to fight, when the bully was tapped on the shoulder. He and his brother wheeled around to see two very unhappy looking people staring right at them: Gabe and Robert.

"Well, what's going on here?" asked Gabe.

"Nothing, and mind your own business!" Melvin shouted.

"Sure, nothing," said Robert. "Hey, Shane, these two giving you problems?"

"Yes," said Shane. "And Gabe, this is the same kid from last year I was telling you about."

"Wait a minute, your name is Gabe?" the older brother asked. "Gabe Rubin?"

"Yes," Gabe nodded.

"And are you Rob Raines?" the older brother asked Robert.

"Indeed," Robert responded.

"You didn't tell me this kid knew Gabe Rubin and Rob Raines," the brother whispered to Melvin.

"What's your name?" Gabe asked, keeping his cool.

"I'm Al," the older brother said. "And this is my brother Melvin."

"What's wrong? Why are you scared?" Melvin asked.

"These two are, like, second degree black belts or something," Al answered. "My friend said they could kill a guy with one punch!"

"Well, Melvin, my brother says that you've been picking on him," Gabe said, ignoring Al's ridiculous commentary. "I don't approve of that."

"And now you are, too, Al? But it looks like you're going to be in our school," Robert said. "Right?"

"Yes, that's true," said Al, shaking.

"Well, you have two choices," Gabe said, patting Al on the shoulder.

"You can either be our best friend, or we can make your life very difficult."

"I'd rather be your friends, if that's OK," Al answered, still shaking.

"Well then, you'd better apologize," said Gabe.

"I'm sorry," Al whimpered.

"Not to us, to him!" Robert said, laughing.

"Sorry," Al said to Shane.

"You, too," Gabe said, nodding at Melvin.

"I'm sorry," Melvin said to Shane.

"It's OK," Shane responded.

"Excellent. Now why don't you get back to your tour?" Gabe suggested.

"Yes, sir," Al said, his head down. Then he ran off in the direction of the cafeteria with Melvin right behind him.

"How'd you guys know I was in trouble?" Shane asked once the bullies had left.

"We didn't," Robert answered. "We were just looking for you to tell you it's lunchtime."

"Oh, cool," said Shane. "That was really cool, by the way. I almost fell apart laughing when the older one found out who you were. How'd you get that kinda reputation?"

"I'm not entirely sure," said Gabe. "I think someone saw us doing Ju-Jitsu one day and spread the word. It's nice, though, because even with Rob's mouth we never have to fight."

"What do you mean 'even with Rob's mouth?'" asked Robert.

"You do have a knack for getting us into trouble," Gabe said. "But luckily I have a knack for getting us out of trouble."

"Oh, whatever," said Robert. "Let's go have lunch, Mister High and Mighty, if you can fit your gigantic head through the door."

The rest of the day passed without any more incidents, but, that night, Jake had a nightmare for the first time in nearly ten years. Usually he slept like a log and snored like a lumberjack, but not that night. Nightmares, Jake knew, were the culmination of subconscious fears. The last one had been about his first day of high school, but this one was far worse. He could see everything in his mind so clearly that he could no longer tell it was, in fact, a dream. He saw himself as the Blue Knight, sword in hand.

Then, upon closer inspection, he could see that his hair had grown long, along with his beard. It looked as though he desperately needed a shower. Upon even closer inspection he saw himself sitting on the side of a busy street, sword in one hand, an almost empty cup in the other. The cup was filled with coins: He could tell by the sound. Then he realized what the dream was; he was seeing himself, homeless, begging for money on the side of the street as the Blue Knight! He woke up in a cold sweat, clutching his blanket. Then, in the silent dark of night, he made the decision that would change everything.

Chapter 9

Gone

Daniel woke up the next morning just knowing it was going to be a good day. For one thing, he had been allowed to wake up on his own, without any dogs licking his face, sorcerers hovering over him, or even the more conventional alarm clock. He was looking forward to his training that morning, now finally feeling back at full strength. Then he was looking forward to a relaxing and fun afternoon with Jake, followed by a romantic evening out with Jamie. Some days, he could actually picture himself marrying that girl. Yes, he thought, his life was finally starting to make complete sense.

Before he knew it, Jake and Robert had shown up, and it was time to train. Their training went especially well that day. Jake was pushing himself particularly hard for some reason, which pushed Daniel to do the same. Gabe caught Daniel's added enthusiasm and passed it on to Robert and Shane. When they finished their training they were all exhausted but feeling good. The younger boys ran off quickly to play video games.

"Excellent training today, boys," Mercury said to Daniel and Jake.

"Yeah, it felt really good," said Daniel.

"Jake, you were working especially hard," said Mercury, looking strangely at Jake. "I'm impressed."

"Yeah," said Jake, looking down.

"Well, see you later," Mercury said in a bizarre tone, and then disappeared.

"Where do you think he goes when he disappears like that?" asked Daniel, laughing.

"I dunno," said Jake, still staring at the ground.

"I mean, you think he goes to some ghost resort, or a giant ghost poker game or something?" Daniel asked. "Or, like, some kind of ghost town?"

"I dunno," Jake responded, still not lifting his head.

Daniel stopped laughing and looked at his friend. "You OK?" he asked.

"Look, there's something I gotta tell you," Jake said.

"What's up?" Daniel asked.

"Last night, I made a decision," Jake said, pausing.

"Congratulations!" Daniel joked. "I'm proud of you."

"No jokes, just listen," Jake said. "Like I said, I made a decision. Being the Blue Knight is not going to help plan my future. I don't wanna end up a Blue Knight bum on some street corner."

"What?" Daniel asked, bewildered.

"I can't do this anymore!" Jake said, suddenly raising his voice, then calming down again. "Look, I know you're not going to understand this, but I'm still able to go to the ROTC training. I'm going to the Marines."

"What?!?" Daniel exclaimed. "You couldn't think of anything else?"

"Nothing else that I wanted to do," Jake answered. "I mean, being a Marine is what I've always wanted to do, for as long as I can remember. You know that better than anyone."

"But I thought you decided to stay here!" Daniel said.

"I changed my mind … again," Jake shrugged. "I mean, we're going nowhere right now! We haven't even been needed in over a month. And even if the Knights are needed, the people will have you to help them."

"So you're just going to turn your back on everything?" Daniel asked. "I mean, we stopped Hellfire! I couldn't have done that without you."

"Hellfire is dead," Jake answered. "The only real enemy the Knights ever had is dead. Now it is time for us to move on."

"There will always be another enemy," Daniel said. "It's not over yet!"

"This is just your childhood fantasy. Our battle is over," Jake said, starting to walk away.

"No, Jake!" Daniel called. "Just stay. I mean, you'll find a plan eventually."

"I can't wait for that to happen," Jake said. He walked out the door, got into his car, and drove away.

Daniel watched Jake pull away, a lump in his throat and tears in his eyes. He had no idea when, or if he would ever see Jake again. His day had just taken a massive turn for the worse. He went upstairs, shut the door, and turned on his headphones.

In his room, the time passed very slowly for Daniel. The TV was on, but he wasn't really watching. He had his computer next to him, but he didn't play any games. He just hung out on his bed, staring up at his ceiling, trying to lose himself in the rock music blaring out of his headphones. He didn't hear the phone ring or his mother call to him. She burst through the door to tell him that the phone was for him.

"Hello," he said grumpily.

"Dan?" came Jamie's voice on the other end.

"Jamie!" Daniel exclaimed, sitting up. "Wow, am I glad it's you."

"Boy, that didn't really sound like you at all!" Jamie said.

"Yeah, I've been having a bad day," he replied. "Jake's gone."

"I know," Jamie said solemnly over the phone. "That's why I'm calling. Liz just called me, really upset. She's really in bad shape; she didn't expect him to break up with her at all."

"What?" Daniel asked. "He broke up with her?"

"Yeah," Jamie answered. "She's really in bad shape, taking it really hard."

"I can imagine," Daniel said. "Hey, I know. Why don't you invite her out with us tonight?"

"That's kinda why I was calling," Jamie answered.

"Oh, yeah it's no problem!" Daniel said, feeling a little better.

"No, that's not what I meant," Jamie said. "I need to spend time just with her tonight. She's really not doing well, I'm kinda worried."

"You're breaking our plans?" Daniel said, a hint of anger in his voice.

"Yeah," Jamie said.

"OK, I … understand," said Daniel. "Well, maybe tomorrow then?"

"Actually, I don't think so," said Jamie. "I kind of need to be with her for the next few weeks."

"But I need you now," Daniel said, becoming more upset. "I need you now as much as she does. He was my best friend, after all. And you had plans with me!"

"Relax! Look, she needs me. I can't believe you'd get angry at me for this!"

"For what, abandoning me when I need you?" Daniel snapped.

"Dan, you have your brothers, and your parents, and Ryan and Jeanne," Jamie responded, getting riled up herself. "Liz has nobody now but me. She is as close to a sister as I've ever had, and so I have to be there for her. You're strong; I know you can get through this."

"But being with you will make it so much easier!" Daniel answered.

"I have to be with her for now," Jamie said. "You can get through this without me; I don't think she can. Be with your brothers, or Ryan or Jeanne today. Go and save somebody's life. Be your own hero."

"I'm sick of being a hero," Daniel said. "I can't believe you're abandoning me."

"For the last time, I'm not abandoning you!" Jamie answered.

"You're letting me down when I really need you. If that isn't abandoning me, then what is?" Daniel said. "You know, you're really not the person I thought you were."

"What are you saying?" Jamie asked.

"I'm saying that if you don't have time for me now, when I need you, then when are you going to have time for me?" Daniel said, a sudden calm in his voice. "I don't need a girlfriend who can't be there for me."

"Oh for God's sakes, Daniel, I told you I can hang out in a few weeks," Jamie said. "Don't do this."

"I'm not doing anything," Daniel said. "You've already done it. I'm just making it official. Maybe next time you meet someone you like you'll pay more attention to him."

"Daniel, be reasonable," Jamie said. "This doesn't have anything to do with you!"

For the second time that day he said good-bye to someone he cared about, and hung up the phone.

He put his head face down in his pillow and cried for the first time since his first day in Paris. He looked outside and saw that it was a beautiful, sunny day. First Jake, then Jamie, and now the weather. Nobody cared about him anymore. He was all alone in a cruel world. He couldn't help but feel sorry for himself as he sat alone in his room. It was there that Shane found him.

"Hey, what time you going out?" Shane asked.

"I'm not," Daniel answered from under his pillow.

"Awesome!" Shane said. "Then you can hang out with us tonight!"

"I guess so," Daniel answered.

"You're not going out?" Lillian asked. "Then can you stay with the boys? Dad and I have plans with Ed and Marie. Robert is staying here, too. They're all pretty upset about Jake leaving. So can you stay and take care of them?"

"Sure, why not?" Daniel answered.

"Thanks," she said.

"Cool," Shane said. "Tonight's gonna be great. Well, I'm gonna get back down there, it's probably my turn again. Come down in a bit, OK?"

"All right," said Daniel.

Daniel stayed on his bed longer than he expected after Shane left. He just didn't feel like getting up. He couldn't believe his day so far: First Jake had left, then Jamie had broken up with him. Not quite the day he had in mind. By the time he forced himself out of bed the sun was going down and his parents had left. When he saw the brilliant fire of the setting sun, Daniel suddenly had an urge to be outside, free from everything and everyone. Instead he fought the urge and joined Gabe, Robert and Shane.

"What are you playing?" he asked as he walked into the room.

"Football," Gabe answered. "If you wait a few minutes this game will be over and we can play four-player."

Daniel sat for only a few minutes. The empty feeling he had inside just wouldn't go away. He tried meditating, but he couldn't clear his head, couldn't force the negative thoughts out. He kept picturing Jake walking away. Jake never had any problem leaving the people he cared about to do what he thought was right for him. Even after all these years, Daniel still had a hard time accepting that fact about his best friend. Then there was the whole thing with Jamie. She had definitely seemed like the one. She was everything he wanted, or at least he had thought so. Was it possible he had made a mistake? He tried to think of the one thing that could help him find his answers.

"I'm gonna go running," he said to the other boys.

"But it's dark outside," Gabe said.

"I'll be careful," Daniel answered.

"Wear bright clothing," Robert said.

"Yeah, and hurry back," Shane said. "I'm on your team when you get back."

"We'll see," Daniel said, walking out of the room.

He quickly got ready and went outside. He started jogging, following a three-mile course around his housing development. Three miles was generally the perfect distance for Daniel. As he hit the corner he cranked up the music in his headphones, let his mind relax, and let his body do all the work.

It felt good to be running. The empty feeling didn't go away, but that wasn't necessarily a bad thing when he was running. He used that feeling to his advantage, using it to fuel his fire. He muscled up the Big Hill with no problem, and kept on going. The more he ran, the less empty he felt. He did the whole course with no problem, and soon saw his house once again.

He stopped in front of his house and looked at it. He knew that his brothers and Robert were in there. He knew that they were waiting for him. The whole course had taken about twenty minutes, and they were probably expecting him back soon. But the thought of going inside and sitting down just made the empty feeling come creeping back. So he turned away from his house to run the course again.

He did the whole course again, and was only a few minutes away from his house when Mercury's voice exploded inside his head. "DANGER!"

Daniel turned up his music, and kept running.

"DANGER!!" came Mercury's voice again, louder than before. Daniel kept running, and turned up the music again.

"You cannot drown out my voice," Mercury said. "It comes from inside of your head. Now stop running and listen to me."

Sorry, thought Daniel. *I'm not in the mood.*

Mercury appeared before him, but he ran right through the ghost.

"Daniel, stop!" Mercury said. "You are needed."

"Sorry, not tonight," said Daniel, stopping. "I'm just not in the mood."

"Not in the mood?" Mercury repeated incredulously.

"I've had a really bad day, and I don't feel like being a hero today," Daniel responded.

"I know about your day, but unfortunately it doesn't work that way," Mercury said. "You can't only be a hero when it's convenient for you."

"I'm only a hero because I have that sword anyway," Daniel said, frowning.

"That's not true," Mercury replied. "You aren't a hero because you have the sword; you have the sword because you are a hero."

"What?" Daniel asked.

"The sword chose you because you are a hero," Mercury said, "like Jamie told you."

"The sword chose me?"

"Certainly," Mercury replied.

"And what about the others?" Daniel said sharply. "It doesn't really seem like they're very good heroes. Jake left, and Hellfire and Hornet weren't exactly the most heroic guys ever. So why were they chosen?"

Mercury smiled. "It seems like you need to worry about yourself right now," he said. "You're willing to throw away everything good in your life because of one bad day? Jake left; that is unfortunate. But to push Jamie away? And your brothers?"

"I didn't push Jamie away," Daniel said. "She abandoned me."

"That is what you wanted to see," Mercury answered. "You stopped trusting her because you felt betrayed by Jake. But what is done is done. Now you are turning your back on your brothers because you had a 'bad day.' They will always be there for you, remember that. And you are also turning your back on the innocent people who need help tonight. You pledged to help others, whatever the cost, whatever the battle."

"Sorry, I'll be a hero tomorrow," Daniel answered. "I just need a night off."

"I'm not going to change your mind?" Mercury frowned.

"Sorry," Daniel shrugged his shoulders. "I just feel like being a regular guy tonight."

"Very well, then I will see you soon," Mercury said, disappearing.

Daniel couldn't help but feel guilty that he hadn't answered the call. Somewhere in that darkness, someone desperately needed him. But that person was a stranger, and he was not in the mood to concern himself with the well-being of strangers. The world had turned its back on him, so now he was going to turn his back on the world. An eye for an eye.

He decided to walk back to his house, his workout having been interrupted. He supposed he wouldn't be pushed to his limits that night. But when he came up to his house he noticed something strange. The front door was open. As he moved closer, he saw a sight that made him freeze in his tracks. It was a red shield trail, and though Daniel didn't understand how it was possible, he knew that something horrible had happened. He ran inside to find Gabe and Robert lying on the living room floor, bruised and beaten.

"What happened?" asked Daniel.

"I'm sorry," Gabe said, struggling to form his words.

"For what?" Daniel asked frantically.

"We tried to stop him," Robert said.

"Stop who?" Daniel asked, getting very nervous.

"Hellfire," Gabe said. "Hellfire is back. I don't know how. But we couldn't stop him."

"Stop him from doing what?" Daniel asked, looking around. "Where's Shane?"

"Hellfire took him," Robert said. "We fought him, but we were no match. I'm so sorry, Dan."

"Don't be sorry, you did your best," Daniel said. "Which is more than I can say about myself."

"He left us alive," Gabe said. "He said he wanted us to give the Knights a message."

"What message?" Daniel asked.

"That if you ever want to see Shane alive again, you'll meet him at the Sunken Meadow Boardwalk," Gabe said. "But you can't go without Jake; you'll be killed."

"I have no choice," Daniel said. "Even if it is …"

"A trap," Mercury interrupted, appearing suddenly.

"You have some nerve showing your face around here!" Daniel said angrily. "You could have told me that it was Shane who was in danger."

"You had made your decision," Mercury said.

"That's a load of crap!" Daniel yelled. "It would have been a different story if …"

"If you knew it was you who was being affected," Mercury said. "Isn't that why you are a hero, because you want to spare others the pain of a loss such as this?"

Daniel froze, Mercury's lesson sinking in. "Fine, you proved your point," he said. "I'm always on call from now on. Still, now Shane is probably going to die because I wasn't here to stop Hellfire."

"No," said Mercury. "The only reason Shane is alive right now is because you weren't here. If you had been here, Hellfire would have killed you, and the other boys as well."

"What does he have against me anyway?" Daniel asked. "Why does he hate me so much?"

"He doesn't," Mercury answered. "He wants your sword."

"He already has one of his own, though," Daniel said. "Why does he want mine?"

"Didn't you notice in your last encounter that he had four gems instead of two?" Mercury asked. "That is because he combined the red and orange swords to form one even more powerful sword."

"Where's Hornet then?" Daniel asked.

"Hellfire killed Hornet after your first encounter," Mercury said. "Once he learned that the swords could be combined, he acquired the closest one to him."

"How did he know the swords could be combined?" Daniel asked. "I never knew that."

"I told him," Mercury said.

"What?!?" Daniel exclaimed.

"I have been advising him," Mercury said. "It was I who told him where he could find you, and it was I that led him here tonight."

"You weasel!" Daniel yelled. "You've been working for him the whole time?"

"No, I don't work for anyone," Mercury answered. "It was also I who made sure you would be out of the house when he arrived. I knew when Jake would have his nightmare, when you would leave, and what you would say when I asked you to help someone. I didn't tell Hellfire Jake was gone, but I told him that the best chance he had was to kidnap Shane. Being able to tell the future helps."

"I don't understand," Daniel answered. "Why do all of this?"

"Since their powers are the same, the swords can be combined. The swords are always being drawn together," Mercury answered. "They would have found each other even without my help. I am sent to be their guide, to make sure that they come together in a way that would be safe for the world."

"Tell me the whole story," said Daniel. "And be quick."

Mercury paused, shook his head, and then lifted up his hand. "No. Let me show you," he said as the room around them dissolved in a brilliant blue flash.

Chapter 10

Mercury

Mercury stumbled out of the forest and into the sunny clearing. Only his tattered brown cloak showed the wear of his long journey. His light gray goatee was still neatly trimmed. The hood of his cloak covered his bald head, but from under the hood his crystal blue eyes were still fierce with determination. He paused, sucked in a deep breath, and continued on toward the castle now towering in front of him.

Each step was wobbly and slow, but he continued moving forward. He paused several times to take deep, labored breaths, fighting back the darkness creeping in from the sides of his eyes. Finally he reached the outside of the castle gate and allowed himself to stop. He opened his mouth to announce his presence, but felt his knees buckle instead. Suddenly, the darkness overwhelmed his vision, and he fell. He barely felt himself hit the ground as he drifted away from consciousness.

He was not at all surprised to wake up hours later, in a plush room inside the castle, to the sound of voices outside of the door. He struggled to hear, but the thick door kept out most of the sound. He closed his eyes, slowed his breathing, and focused. Inside of his mind a picture emerged. He saw a small boy with freckled cheeks and reddish brown hair, holding the hand of an old knight. The old knight was large and well fed, and his own reddish brown hair was flecked with gray. The old knight was talking to a younger knight with dark hair and a powerful build. Mercury focused harder, and finally the conversation became audible.

"How many men did we lose in the latest attack, Leopold?" The old knight asked.

"Sixty, Sir Samuel," the young knight responded.

"We do not have enough men to be losing sixty at every battle!" Sir Samuel said. "You train these men, and you lead them into battle. What can we do? How can I change this?"

"I do not know, sire," Leopold shook his head. "Our men are well trained, and they are brave in battle. However, Henry's men greatly outnumber our own forces. We cannot defend against such overwhelming numbers. Frankly, sir, we need a miracle."

Sir Samuel held his son's hand tightly, shook his head, and opened the door to Mercury's room.

"Ahh, you are awake!" Sir Samuel said, smiling. "When we found you outside unconscious, we took you in here. We figured that you could use some rest."

"Thank you," Mercury said. "That was much needed."

"You are welcome," Sir Samuel replied. "Now, exactly who are you and where did you come from?"

"Well, my name is Mercury," Mercury answered. "As for where I come from, the answer is nowhere and everywhere. I am a wanderer, looking for those kind enough to harbor me for a short time. I am a sorcerer."

"A sorcerer?" exclaimed Sir Samuel. "I thought sorcerers were nothing but fairytales."

"Well, sir, I am one of a select few of my kind," Mercury replied. "I work specifically in the arts of bringing joy and promoting happiness."

"How can we be sure that you are who you say you are?" asked Leopold.

"Leopold!" shouted Sir Samuel. "How dare you insult our guest?"

"Do not scold him, please," interjected Mercury. "He was only watching out for your safety. It was a valid question. Do not worry, my good Sir Leopold, with our host's permission I shall give a small demonstration."

"By all means," Sir Samuel nodded.

Mercury smiled and turned to the boy. "And what is your name?"

"Ramsey," the boy said quietly. "How do you do?"

Mercury smiled, though he sensed something strange about the boy. "I am well, thank you. How old are you?"

"I am seven years," replied Ramsey.

"Seven, eh? That is a good age. Hmm …" Mercury paused, tapping his chin, seeming to think of something very important. "Ah, yes, now I have it. Here, this is for you." He held out his hand, and a pale blue light came out of it. It formed into a ball, and then the ball formed into a small wooden sword.

The boy's eyes widened, and a smile formed on his lips. "Thank you, Mercury!"

Sir Samuel laughed. "Well, will you look at that? You're just full of surprises, eh, Mercury? All right Ramsey, off to bed."

Ramsey smiled as he ran off to his nurse, swinging the sword in front of him.

"Adorable child. He is the image of his father," Mercury said. "But now I would like to go back to sleep, if you do not mind. I am afraid I am still weary from my journey."

"Of course," said Sir Samuel. "Make yourself at home, and you are welcome here as long as you like."

"Thank you very much," replied Mercury. "You really are too kind. I am in your debt."

Mercury sank into the plush bed, drifted to sleep, and began his life in Sir Samuel's town. He enjoyed living in the town, so much so that in the blink of an eye two years had passed. With a heavy heart, he realized that it was time again for him to move on. But he did not want to leave without repaying his host for all the kindness shown to him. He wanted to give a gift, something unique and splendid, something fitting the place that the sorcerer wished he could call home. A sudden gift idea popped into his head, and he smiled at his own brilliance. He found Sir Samuel and broke the news of his departure, and told Sir Samuel that he would be giving a gift. The lord nodded, and asked the sorcerer to present it at a farewell ceremony that evening.

Then Mercury headed back to his room and carefully lowered to his knees. He closed his eyes, and took a few deep breaths, getting himself ready for the task ahead. He placed his hands out in front of him, palms facing about shoulder width apart. Soon sweat started to wet his brow, and his face began to twitch as if he were in pain.

An electric blue line formed between his hands at the center of the palms, no thicker than a blade of grass. He gritted his teeth as the line grew thicker and brighter. He did not even realize that he was flexing all the muscles of his body and his breath was rapid and labored. He forced his hands together, struggling against his own power. When his hands finally touched, a brilliant blue light filled the room. The light vanished; he opened his eyes and looked into his hands. He let out a deep sigh of relief, and let fall to the floor four bright gems. They were each of a different color: green, blue, orange, and red.

He placed the four gems in front of him in a row, and placed his palms on top of them. From under his hands the same blue light could be seen, this time lasting only a few seconds. When Mercury removed his hands there were now eight gems. Each of the four bright gems now had an opposite, a dark gem of the same color. Mercury looked, then nodded, picked up the gems, and headed off for the ceremony.

When he arrived he found not only Sir Samuel waiting for him, but everyone who lived in and around the castle. The crowd hushed as he approached, waiting for the sorcerer to speak.

"As you may already know," said Mercury. "I am going to leave here this evening."

At this the crowd booed and shouted their unhappiness. "No, stay!" "Please, Mercury, stay!" "Don't leave!" came the shouts from the crowd. Mercury just held up his hands, and silence once again fell over the assembly.

"I have had a wonderful time here. I have never called any place home, but if I had that luxury, this would be it. You are all very good people, and it pains me to leave you." He paused, took a deep sentimental breath, and then continued. "But I wish to bestow upon all of you a gift.

Sir Samuel, this is when I give you my full power. Please, have your four strongest knights step forward."

Sir Samuel consulted Leopold, who quickly ran off and picked the four best knights. They each stepped forward, armor gleaming in the late afternoon sun.

Mercury held up his hands, and a brilliant blue light filled the air. When the light cleared, four swords rested on top of four shields on the table in front of Mercury. "Step up to a sword," Mercury said. They did as they were told. "Thank you, and now for this." From his cloak he pulled the eight gems. On each sword he placed two of the same color. He placed them on opposite sides of the hilt just above the blade. When this was finished he quickly shot his hands up, and the entire town jumped back. His hands sparked, and blue lightning bolts shot from his palms to each sword. The bolts sped up, and then jumped to all four swords at once. He held this for a moment, then the lightning vanished and he dropped his hands.

"Well, knights, come and claim your equipment!" said Mercury, looking very pleased with his work.

The knights looked at him in disbelief. "Go on, do not fear," Mercury said again.

The first knight approached his sword, which now held the orange gems. He looked at it, and saw that the gems had become fixed to their hilts by Mercury's lightning bolts. As he drew closer, the bright orange gem began to glow. Soon the bright orange glow filled the entire sword. The knight curiously reached out and grabbed the hilt. As he did, the bright light shot through him and then filled the air around him. When the light subsided, the knight's silver armor was streaked with bright orange. The knight looked curiously at the sword as he moved it about.

"It feels lighter," he said.

"Oh, no, it is the same weight, you are just stronger," said Mercury, smiling.

At this, the other three knights approached their swords, which all started to glow like the orange sword had. One by one they grabbed their swords, and the air was filled with red, green, and blue. When they were finished they stood there, each with armor brightly streaked with the color of their gems. They moved their new swords about, feeling their new strength and speed, for they had indeed grown faster as well. The blue knight, with full armor on, decided to see how fast he could run. He found that he could run faster than any horse. At this, the green knight ran to catch him, and found that his speed had increased as well.

"Fascinating!" cried Sir Samuel, leaping from his chair.

Mercury smiled. "You asked for a means to defend your people. Well, here it is. These four are your miracle."

"Thank you! Thank you so much! Yes, this is what we need, the miracle we have been searching for!" Sir Samuel replied, extending his hand. "Until our paths cross again."

Mercury took his hand and said, "Yes, I hope that day comes soon. Use the gift I have given you wisely."

Ramsey ran up and gave Mercury a big hug. Mercury picked up the young boy and held him in his arms for a second. "Mercury, please do not go!" Ramsey pleaded.

"Do not worry, Ramsey," Mercury said. "We will meet again."

He began to walk away, then stopped and turned. "Oh, and one more thing! The swords can change holders in one of three ways. The first is through natural death, in which case the sword will choose an heir. The second way is as a gift. And the third way is through defeat."

And with that he walked off, vanishing into the forest as quickly and mysteriously as he had arrived two years before. Sir Samuel looked down at Ramsey, then at the four knights, and smiled broadly once again. They walked back to the castle together.

That night the attack came, and the knights had their first test. Henry's force was larger than ever before. The entire town gathered to see Mercury's knights in action.

"Samuel!" cried Sir Henry, leading the attacking troops. "Samuel! Surrender or send a force to stop me!"

Sir Samuel went out with the four knights to speak with Henry. "Please, take your troops and leave our land. We do not wish to fight."

"Of course you do not wish to fight," Henry scoffed. "You can always surrender your land and your people."

"We cannot surrender," Sir Samuel replied.

"Then we will settle this in battle!" Henry retorted.

The knights immediately stepped in front of Sir Samuel, who turned around to ride back inside the walls. As he was riding Henry called for the first volley of arrows. Leopold pushed Ramsey behind his back, but Ramsey peeked his head around just as the arrow hit its mark, just above Sir Samuel's armor at the neck. Sir Samuel slouched forward in the saddle as the horse rode through the gate. The drawbridge closed and the battle began—four knights against an attacking squad of two hundred and eighty seven soldiers, to be exact.

"Sire, are you all right?!?" Leopold asked, rushing down the stairs.

"Must ... see ... battle," Sir Samuel managed to say, blood dribbling out of his mouth.

"Yes, of course, sire," Leopold said, amazed that the old knight was still alive.

Leopold and another knight helped Sir Samuel up to the ramparts in time to witness the majority of the battle. The sun had already been down for hours, but the moon gave enough light to see almost perfectly. Sir Samuel could see through the growing haze in his vision that the four knights were not being overwhelmed. He understood almost immediately that he did not have to send his other forces.

The green knight took command, ordering the orange knight to begin taking out the catapults. The orange knight sprinted toward the catapults, and before Sir Henry's men knew it, he had destroyed a catapult with one swing of his sword. Before the splinters even hit the ground, the other three catapults were destroyed. The green knight told the red knight to take out the archers, which was done instantly. The blue knight took out the horses as the green knight went after the attackers on foot. In less than ten minutes the battle was over, and Sir Samuel's town was saved. Sir Henry gathered up what remained of his forces and fled into the woods.

"We ... are ... saved," Sir Samuel managed to say. "Thank ... you ... Mercury ... my friend."

"Father, we have done it! Mercury's gifts, they saved us! They saved us all!" Ramsey waited for a reply, but none came. "Father?"

Ramsey looked up to see his father's eyes closed, and his head hanging forward. "Father? No, please, father, we are all saved! You cannot leave now, we are all saved!"

Ramsey felt the tears welling up, and did not bother to wipe them away. He had never known his mother; his father was all that he had. Now he was watching his father leave him forever. Ramsey began to cry uncontrollably as his whole world vanished.

"Come, Master Ramsey, we must go," Leopold said, as he took Ramsey and walked away

Twelve years later, Ramsey had finished his training as a knight, and Leopold was proud of the man that Ramsey had become. He had always looked on Ramsey as a nephew, and he could not help but feel the pride that an uncle feels for a successful nephew. The town prospered as it never had before because Ramsey had not been shy in using his knights to invade and pillage nearby towns. Leopold had not been thrilled by this behavior, for it was unlike Sir Samuel, but he felt that the happiness the townspeople enjoyed was worth the change. On the outside, Ramsey seemed like a great ruler.

But Ramsey was not content. He knew by now that his army was the greatest in England; if he had wanted he could most likely challenge for the throne. But he was not happy with only the most powerful army. He still did not have any power himself; the power lay in his army of four knights with their magical swords. He knew that loyalties could change easily, and if someone could come along and turn the four knights against him, he was powerless. He remembered Mercury's words of how the swords could change holders. The knights were old, but they were not near death. And Ramsey knew that, while he was a good fighter, he could not defeat the knights as long as they held the power. But he knew the knights' only weakness: their loyalty. He knew that they would do whatever was asked of them, and so he decided to demand one of the swords as a gift.

He approached the four knights, who were training in the courtyard. When they saw him they all stopped and knelt in his presence.

"Sire, how may we be of service?" asked the green knight.

"My old friends," Ramsey began. "You served my father well, and saved our town the night he died. Since then you have served me well, bringing glory to our small but great town. I now ask only one more favor of you."

"Sire?" replied the knights, standing.

"I wish for one of you to bestow your sword upon me as a gift," said Ramsey, turning to the green knight and holding out his hand. "Please, great warrior, a gift for your feudal lord."

"It is to you, Lord Ramsey," the green knight said reluctantly, "that I bestow this green sword. It is my gift to my feudal lord." He knelt down as he said this, with the sword resting on his outstretched hands.

Ramsey looked at the sword, his mouth watering. As he reached for it, the sword began to glow with a dark green light. He grabbed the handle, and the light shot through him and into the air. When the light vanished, Ramsey's armor was streaked with a dark, almost sad green. He looked at himself, and then at the sword, and then he let out a horrible laugh.

"Yes! This is incredible! This power, I cannot believe it!" He continued to laugh, but then stopped abruptly. He looked at the former green knight still on his knees. "You, you who have granted me with this power, what reward shall I give to you?"

The knight straightened up and prepared to speak, but Ramsey interrupted him. "I know! You shall be the first to taste my new power!"

The red knight ran up. "Sire, please ..." he began.

"Stay out of this!" Ramsey shouted, not even glancing at the red knight.

The other knights could only look on in horror as Ramsey quickly lowered the sword, and the former green knight was no more. Ramsey stood over the body, seeing blood on his sword for the first time. He felt a kind of power he never had before, the power to end life. He had had power over armies and towns, but now he had power for himself, and he liked it. He stood quivering from the power, and a realization hit him. There were others as powerful as he was, and if they banded together he could be defeated. He could not allow this.

He turned his head and with a wicked grin looked at the red knight.

Ramsey advanced on this knight and said to him, "You. You attempted to stop me, did you not? Yes, you desired the power all for yourself! You are a traitor!"

The red knight had his back pressed up against the wall. His knees began to shake and give way underneath him. Suddenly, with all the force left in him, he leapt forward and attacked. Ramsey parried the attack with ease. The red knight fought with the wisdom and experience of a seasoned warrior, but the much younger and naturally stronger Ramsey was able to outmaneuver him. Ramsey always parried his strikes, and was always a step ahead of his feints. Soon, the former red knight was no more.

The blue and orange knights just stared, too afraid to bring themselves to move. When Ramsey had defeated his second enemy he unsheathed the green sword, and looked at both blades. Having defeated both former holders, he reasoned, he should now control both swords. But, for some reason, he was no more powerful with two blades than he was with one. He saw the gems, and realized that they were the secret.

And so he tried to place the two swords together so that the gems would touch. But he found that he could not make the swords touch, no matter how hard he tried. He looked down and realized that he had been trying to touch the dark green gem to the light red gem. So he flipped both swords so that the dark gems were facing each other. The gems almost pulled themselves together. As they touched, there was a spark, followed by a flash of light. The two swords glowed fiercely, and became one. Ramsey looked at the sword as the glow subsided. On one side of the new sword were the dark green and red gems, on the other side were the bright ones. Ramsey walked up to the floating sword and reached out to grip the handle. It stopped floating and fell into his hand.

He gripped the sword, and as he did he was hit by a fierce wind. His rich auburn hair flew back, his arms flew up slightly, and his head was thrown back. The wind stayed on him for a few seconds before it died down, and he fell to one knee, gasping for breath. It was then that the other two knights, courage fully mustered, chose to attack him.

Since Ramsey's outward appearance had not changed, they thought that he was actually weakened by the strange events, and so it was the optimal time to attack. If he had been weakened, then together they could defeat him easily. They rushed forward at full speed. Ramsey, still on one knee, looked up and saw them coming, seemingly helpless to do anything about it. They brought their swords down together. They were surprised to find, however, that their cuts did not follow through. In fact, the swords stopped so quickly and so violently that the knights were stunned. They looked down, and saw that their blades had been effortlessly blocked.

They began with all of their strength to push against Ramsey's sword, but he easily returned to his feet. Once he was on his feet, he pushed against their blades and sent them both stumbling back. The fact was that his new sword had made him even more than twice as powerful as he had been. He quickly vanquished the blue and orange knights, and their swords fell to the ground.

Soon the orange sword was part of his arsenal, and then he knelt down to add the blue sword as well. As he touched the dark blue gem to the others, he saw the same sight he had seen the first two times. The four swords were separate, and then turned into pure light. They moved together, this time blinking with all four colors. The ground began to shake as the blinking sped up. Clouds filled the sky, and rain began to fall. A streak of lightning was quickly followed by a crack of thunder. The wind picked up, driving so hard that the trees in the courtyard bent until they nearly broke. The sword began to blink black and white. Then, suddenly, all was quiet. The sky lightened, the wind died down, and all that was left was the sword. It fell, and the blade stuck into the ground below it.

Ramsey walked up, and could hardly believe what he saw. Instead of a sword with eight gems, he found only two. One gem was bright silver, and the other was dark gray. Curious, Ramsey reached out and gripped the handle. As he did, a sudden darkness fell over him. A dark gray wave ran over him and changed his armor. Instead of being the normal bright metallic color, it changed to black. And where the dark green had been it was now streaked with a dark gray, hardly distinguishable from the black armor. He felt his new power, which was beyond his wildest dreams. It was the kind of power he had dreamed of since the day his father died.

He longed to test this power, to let the entire world know that he was the most powerful. He sheathed the sword at his hip, and walked inside to make his plans.

He walked into the great hall to find Leopold sitting alone. As Ramsey walked in, Leopold looked in wonder at the new armor, and the new sword in its scabbard.

"Sire, is everything all right?" asked Leopold.

"Better than ever," Ramsey replied with a dark sarcasm in his voice. "We go to war. I will lead the troops."

"Sire, you lead the troops?" asked Leopold. "What of the four knights?"

Ramsey looked at him with a fierce glare. "The knights were traitors. They tried to assassinate me. So I dealt with them. I will lead, and you will join me. We will begin with Henry's land, and move on from there. We will conquer all of England in my name! We ride tomorrow."

With that he walked away, and Leopold was left alone to think. He understood what Ramsey had meant about the knights. He suddenly knew what must have happened, and what the new armor must have been. Ramsey's heart was dark, and he needed to be stopped. He also knew that he had neither the power nor the heart to take on his young lord himself. So, without Ramsey knowing, Leopold sent a scout to the Henry's town to warn of the impending danger.

The next day Ramsey set out at the head of his troops, with Leopold at his side. Not being sure of his full power, he had ordered all of his subjects onto the battlefield. There were seven hundred in all. Leopold rode behind Ramsey, all the while trying to hide his contempt. He hoped with all of his heart that the messenger had gotten through, and that together they would be able to stop Ramsey. As they left the town walls Leopold's heart leapt. Henry's army stood on the field in front of the town, ready for battle. The messenger had done his job.

Ramsey saw this and wheeled around. "This was your doing!" he shouted at Leopold. "You wish to stop me? You would be a traitor? Traitors MUST BE DEALT WITH!" he shouted, and with that he raised his sword.

All were watching as he cut down Leopold. Leopold had been their ruler, their mentor, and in many cases their friend. The soldiers became angry, having felt more loyalty toward their teacher and mentor than their current ruler. Their anger begin to boil over, some because Ramsey was their enemy, some because they had seen him kill a loved one, some because he had betrayed them. As one they followed Leopold's last wish, and rushed in to attack Ramsey.

Fifteen hundred people filled the battlefield, and they were all fighting against one man. With each attacker, Ramsey realized more of his power. He was so fast that even though dozens were attacking him at a time, it felt as though they were attacking him one by one. He had achieved his ultimate power, and knew that he could not be stopped. Almost in response to his realization of power, it started to rain. Soon he stood alone in the field; he had defeated all of them. When he looked around and saw that he was alone, he threw back his head and let out a roar, like a hungry lion at his first bite of flesh. It was then that a hooded figure walked silently toward him across the battlefield.

"I see a lot has changed in twelve years," said the figure. "And you certainly have changed, Ramsey."

Ramsey looked at him. "Who are you?" he growled. "How do you know me? Show your face, or you will find yourself joining the others that lay here."

"This grass is stained with blood," said the figure as though he had not heard Ramsey's threat. "It is blood that you have spilled. This pains me dearly to say, but you, Ramsey, must be stopped."

Ramsey growled again, "Who are you?"

The figure threw off his hood, revealing himself as Mercury. "Yes," he said as a shocked look came to Ramsey's face. "I have returned because my gifts have been twisted, and I must stop that from happening. No evil will be my doing."

Ramsey laughed. "How can you stop me? I control the swords, your ultimate creations. You could not possibly stop me."

"You are wrong on two counts," Mercury replied. "I can stop you, and you do not fully control the swords."

Ramsey stopped laughing and looked at the sorcerer. "What do you mean?"

Mercury did not reply. Instead he threw the front of his cloak back over his shoulders, and raised his hand so the palm faced Ramsey. The sword that Ramsey held glowed bright silver in response. The glow increased, and the sword separated in two. Ramsey still held the sword with the dark gray gem, but the silver gem was gone. His sword was only a shadow of the one he had just been holding; there was no light left in it. The other form was the soul of the sword, which glowed silver and flew into Mercury's hands.

As Mercury grabbed the sword, the glow went away. It was exactly the same as the sword Ramsey was holding, except that on one side there was the silver gem. On the opposite side there was nothing.

Ramsey laughed. "Ha! And to think I was almost frightened with all of that nonsense. I am no less powerful than before, and you are no different. You cannot defeat me!"

"You are wrong," replied Mercury. "You are no less powerful, that is true. But I am now even more powerful than you! Now I give you this chance: Plant your sword in the ground and renounce your evil ways."

Ramsey laughed menacingly, and then darted at Mercury, running full force straight at the old sorcerer. Mercury merely stood in the same position, looking as if he were completely unaware of the threat on its way. As Ramsey rushed at Mercury, the young knight pulled his arm back, readying his sword for the fatal blow. Mercury still made no movement. Ramsey came forward, swinging his arm across his body as hard as he could, aiming to slash the sorcerer's chest. Just before the sword was set to land, however, it was met by its nemesis. They clanged, and the two men held positions for a second, staring each other straight in the eyes. Then Ramsey pulled back, and lunged forward again for another strike. This, too, was blocked, and Ramsey jumped back again. The two warriors stood facing each other, the rain affecting neither.

Mercury made the next move. He leapt forward on the attack, and Ramsey was surprised to find that despite his adversary's age the attacks were quite powerful. They exchanged strike after strike, slash after slash, covering great distances in short amounts of time. The movements were incredibly fast, almost faster than the eye could see. Both handled the heavy hand-and-a-half swords as though they were made of straw, and several times both came close to being struck a final blow. But each was narrowly evaded, and the fight went on.

Each time their swords clashed, thunder shook the air. As the intensity of their fight grew, so did the fury of the storm. It seemed as though the earth itself was being affected by the clash. The rain was now lashing into the two warriors, pelting Ramsey's armor and Mercury's cloak. The driving wind turned the rain sideways. The sky was dark as night. The thunder was right on top of them; each crack was an explosion above their heads. The sky was constantly lit up with flashes of lightning. But for all of this, the two warriors showed no sign that they even noticed the driving storm, and the fury continued to rise.

At last, as the storm became a hurricane, Mercury jumped back. He was breathing heavily. Facing his opponent, Mercury raised the silver gem to his face and closed his eyes.

He spoke aloud to the gem. "The fight must end now. Ramsey must not be allowed to win. I need all of your power. Together we must stop this evil. I must atone for the evil that I have unleashed on this world. We must stop Ramsey now!"

He opened his eyes into the pouring rain. The sword began to glow silver. Ramsey's sword began to glow a dark, sad gray. Then, for the final time, they rushed at one another with battle cries that rose above the storm. As they clashed, thunder shook the air and ground once more, and lightning flashed as though the sun itself was underneath the clouds. For a moment, the entire field was covered with the blinding flash. Then all was dark, and all was quiet. The clouds began to part.

Daniel and the others blinked as the vision around them faded, and they returned to reality.

"That was when I was sent back in this form as the guide and guardian of the swords," Mercury continued. "I knew that they could be dangerous if left together so I moved them: two to Paris and two to Rome, where they sat for almost a thousand years. Most of this part, though, you know."

"But I don't understand the whole Shadow Sword, Soul Sword thing," said Daniel.

"When I created the swords I knew that, if combined, they would be unstoppable," said Mercury. "Since they were all created with my magic, there was no way to stop them from being able to be combined. So I put in a failsafe: the gems. There are two gems on each sword: one dark, one light. The dark represents the human nature to seize everything for one's self. The light represents the human nature to give to others. Both of these are inherent in all humans, with one being the dominant nature. Since this was the case, it ensured that a person could only control one gem at a time, depending on which nature was stronger within him. That way no one person can control all of the power at once. When all four swords are combined they create either the Shadow Sword or the Soul Sword, depending on which nature the holder favors. The other sword remains dormant within, however, waiting to be called out to neutralize the first power."

"So all I have to do is call out the Soul Sword and I can defeat Hellfire?" Daniel asked.

"Not exactly," Mercury said. "First, the dormant nature can only be called out when the four swords have been combined, which would mean that you would need Jake to be here. Also, should you succeed in forming the Soul Sword, it will always be the exact opposite of the Shadow Sword, so when the two face each other, both holders will inevitably be destroyed, and the swords will return to normal. I'm sorry, but in order to save your brother, and the world, you will have to sacrifice yourself, Daniel."

"So be it," Daniel said after a short pause. His face was tense. "Anything to save Shane."

"So this is what you've been planning all along?" Gabe asked. "That Daniel dies?"

"Unfortunately. I had to make sure the world was safe," Mercury said. "I was becoming quite fond of you, too."

"Save it," Daniel replied coldly.

"That's crap," Robert said. "I find it hard to believe that the only way to save Shane is for Dan to die. That's a double-edged sword if I ever heard one."

"Well, I'm not dead yet," said Daniel. "Maybe there'll be a way for me to live through this. Even if you think you know the future, surprises can happen. I'm certainly not going to just lay back and accept my fate in either case. I'm going to go to the Boardwalk and fight Hellfire until I use every last ounce of strength I have. I don't care what you say; I'm going to live long enough to see Shane get to safety. And hopefully even longer."

"Hell, yeah!" Gabe said. "You're not going to give up, ever. You better promise me that."

"I promise," Daniel said. "No matter what the odds, I promise that I will never give up."

"You better not give up," Gabe said. "And I'm coming along to make sure of that."

"No, you aren't," Daniel said.

"Not without me, anyway," Robert said.

"It's too dangerous," Daniel said. "I can't allow it. I won't allow it."

"Hey, we're the ones who let that creep take Shane," Gabe answered. "I don't care how much stronger than me you are, you tell me I can't come along to help rescue my little brother again and I'll kick your butt."

Daniel looked at them and smiled. They were no longer teenagers, but stone-faced warriors, determined to fight. They were bruised and beaten already, but that wouldn't stop them. They were going to help him get Shane back, or die trying.

"Fine," Daniel said at last.

"Now remember, you are at a huge disadvantage," Mercury said. "If you can get Shane back without having to fight, that would be advisable."

"Yeah, you don't have to tell me twice," Daniel answered. "Now can't you, like, give me the blue sword, too? That way I can even out with Hellfire?"

"It is not mine to give," Mercury said. "If the swords were mine to give, I'd have taken the red sword away from Hellfire long ago. I am their guide, not their master. They have no master, remember that. The swords choose their own destinies, as I hope you will. Now go, my friends. May we meet again."

"You're not coming?" asked Daniel.

"I would be of no help," said Mercury. "I must remain neutral, unfortunately. This matter can only be resolved without me. Now your sword and shield are waiting outside."

"Excellent," said Daniel. "And I'll carry these two."

"Let's go kick some butt!" Robert said.

"Yeah, let's make Hellfire sorry that he ever crossed paths with us!" said Gabe.

"He'll regret ever challenging the Knights," Daniel said.

"We get to be Knights?" Gabe asked.

"Tonight you are," Daniel answered. "If you haven't proven yourselves worthy, then who ever could?"

"Awesome!" said Robert.

"So, Knights, we ready to save the world?" Daniel asked.

"Yeah!" Gabe and Robert shouted together.

Chapter 11

Final Fight

"Last chance to stay here," Daniel said.

"Not a chance," Gabe said. "Shane is my little brother, too. All I need is to land one good kick on that jerk and I'll be happy."

Daniel grabbed Gabe and Robert, one under each arm, and flew off. They were headed toward the Sunken Meadow Boardwalk, a small beach on the north shore of Long Island. It overlooked a small body of water called the Long Island Sound. The beach was closed off at night, so they would be the only ones there. Daniel wondered if that was why Hellfire had chosen the location.

"I wish I could call her and apologize," Daniel said as they flew.

"Call who?" Robert asked.

"Jamie," Daniel answered. "She told me she needed to be there for Liz, and I broke up with her."

"You did what?" Gabe asked. "Why would you break up with her? I mean, you two were great together!"

"I don't know why I did it," said Daniel. "I let anger get the best of me, I guess. I was so mad that Jake left. For a second I forgot that her loyalty was one of the things I like so much about her. But now I can't apologize. Gabe, can you do something for me?"

"Yeah, sure," Gabe answered.

"At my funeral, tell her I was sorry," Daniel said.

"Why don't you live through this," Gabe responded, "and tell her yourself?"

"Yeah, you better not die," Robert said. "If you die I'm gonna be real pissed at you."

"I'll do my best," Daniel said, though his tone was not very reassuring.

They landed on the boardwalk, but no one was there. They checked up and down the whole length of the mile-long boardwalk, but found nothing. No signs of life, no traces of either Shane or Hellfire.

"OK, so what now?" Robert asked.

"He did say the Boardwalk, right?" asked Daniel.

"Yeah," Gabe said. "Like, five times."

"Well, then, let's keep looking, I guess," Daniel shrugged.

Gabe and Robert ran along the ground as Daniel flew high overhead. From the air he caught a glimpse of something on the beach, right near the water. When he looked closer he could see that it was Hellfire. He saw no sign of Shane as he swept down toward the spot, signaling Gabe and Robert to join him.

A thousand scenarios were running through Daniel's mind, and none of them seemed promising. As he got closer, however, Hellfire jumped down into a hole in the sand. Daniel hadn't seen the hole before because the night was so dark. He descended slowly after Hellfire, stopping at the entrance to the cave to wait for Gabe and Robert to catch up. The hole was deep, at least fifteen feet. When he finally reached the bottom, Daniel was surprised to see a cave extending in front of him. He saw the red shield trail, and followed it.

The strange cave seemed unnatural to Daniel. The first thing he noticed was that it was made of solid rock, which was strange to find only fifteen feet under a beach. Then, as they were going through, he also noticed that the way it was built made it impossible to walk through, with sudden drops and pitfalls in the ground. It was difficult to fly through as well, with stalactites coming out of the ceiling, some touching the ground. But they were not made of minerals like most stalactites; they were made of solid rock, which also told Daniel that it was man-made. Hellfire had obviously been busy in his month off. The ride through the cave was not a short one, especially for Gabe and Robert. First of all, they were being carried under one of Daniel's arms, and he was holding them tight. Each time they had to avoid an obstacle, Daniel could only see it at the last second, so they were violently swung around until the Green Knight could get his bearings again. On more than one occasion during that ride Gabe had to force himself not to throw up.

As they were riding, however, they noticed something very strange. As they flew through the cave, they noticed that *they could see the red trail in front of them*. They had heard Mercury tell Daniel and Jake about the trails, so they knew what they were, although they had never been able to see them. But there was no mistaking that they could indeed see the red trail, and if they looked behind them they could see the green trail as well. It took their minds completely off of the motion sickness. What could it mean that they saw the trails? Didn't Mercury say that only sword holders could see the trails?

About ten minutes later, their thoughts were cut short as they reached their destination. As it turned out, the cave led to a very extensive chamber at its other end. It was wide and tall, almost like a dome. It was at least fifty feet high, with bright artificial lights. Daniel knew they had not seen it before because it was under the water in the middle of the sound. On one side of the dome was a small scaffolding about four feet long by two feet wide. It was suspended about five feet from the ground by long metal chains, one on each side. There were similar scaffoldings at different levels and different places all the way up to the top of the dome. Daniel guessed that they were somehow used for Hellfire's training. That, or Hellfire had taken up painting on the side. On the opposite side from the first scaffolding was a large throne, on which Hellfire had seated himself.

"I suppose you want to know how I survived," Hellfire said.

"I don't really care," Daniel answered. "I just want my brother back."

"Well, I shall tell you anyway," said Hellfire, rising. "It's really not a long story. My foot was jarred loose when I hit the water. I swam to shore, making sure you couldn't see me."

"You're right," said Daniel. "That wasn't much of a story. Now give me my brother!"

"So uptight," said Hellfire with a wicked smile. "I'll get to that. But let me finish my story first. I was alive, but beaten. It seemed that even though power was on my side, skill and luck were on your side. Not a good combination to have against me. So I set about trying to find the best way to acquire your sword. I obviously couldn't beat you, even with the element of surprise. So I built this place, and used it to train myself until skill was no longer on your side. Then I decided to acquire a trump card—something that would make you lose before you even thought about fighting. Looks as though I chose the right something."

"You can make yourself sound as smart as you want," said Daniel. "But I know the sorcerer was helping you. Just give me my brother back; you have me here, so let him go free."

"Not so fast," said Hellfire. "You see, that child is quite valuable. I'd say he's worth at least two swords. Yet I see only one. Where is the blue sword?"

"What's the matter, I'm not good enough for you?" asked Daniel, grinning.

"Ah, so you came alone," Hellfire sneered. "Not wise. First, that means that you cannot trade for the boy. Second, it means that you are all alone, and no match for me!"

With that he rushed at Daniel. Daniel reached for his sword, but before he could get to it Hellfire's fist was in his stomach. He crumpled to his knees, where he met Hellfire's foot in his face. He flew back and slammed into the smooth stone wall of the dome.

Robert rushed in first and threw a punch at Hellfire, who simply moved out of the way. Then, as Robert was falling forward, Hellfire stuck out his foot, tripping him and sending him face first onto the floor. Gabe also tried his luck by throwing a kick to Hellfire's ribs, but Hellfire was unaffected by the kick. He grabbed Gabe's foot on its way down and sent him sprawling next to Robert.

Next it was Daniel's turn, and he leapt forward. He threw his hardest kicks and punches, but his opponent blocked them all. Hellfire was enjoying seeing Daniel struggle, and gave him a hard shot to the chest. Daniel stumbled back a few steps, then took out his sword and jumped forward. His strike was easily deflected, and without remembering exactly what had happened, he found himself on the floor.

Hellfire lifted him by the throat and in a menacing tone said, "Where is the blue sword?"

"I don't know," Daniel said through the tightening grip on his throat.

"WHERE IS THE BLUE SWORD?" Hellfire repeated loudly, shaking the walls.

"I told you, I don't know," Daniel said, choking. "But even if I did I wouldn't tell you."

"Fine, then, I'll find it myself," said Hellfire. He dropped Daniel, then swung his sword down hard at the hero. It clanged to a halt.

"There will be no need for that," a familiar voice said. "The blue sword is here."

"Jake!" Daniel exclaimed, looking up.

"Sorry I'm late," said Jake. "Traffic was murder. I got caught behind this ninety-year-old lady who could barely stand on her shield."

Daniel laughed, then asked, "How did you know what was going on?"

"Mercury showed up and explained everything," he said. "I came as soon as I could, which almost wasn't soon enough."

"Yeah, I was almost a lot shorter," Daniel said.

"Well, now all four swords are here," Hellfire said. "I love family reunions."

"That's right," said Jake as Gabe and Robert walked up behind him. "There's no way you can beat us."

"I'm not so sure about that," said Hellfire. "But in any case, I'm not even going to waste my time trying. Have you forgotten that I have a very special bargaining chip?"

"Shane," said Daniel. "Where is he?"

"Ah, wait, you must understand the rules first," said Hellfire. "Rule number one: If you try to attack me, he dies. Rule number two: Try anything funny, he dies. Rule number three: If this doesn't go exactly as I say, he dies."

"Just show us the kid," said Jake.

Hellfire walked over to his throne and pushed a button on one of the armrests. A few feet to the left of the throne a panel opened up in the floor, and a small cage rose up. Inside of the cage, unharmed but frightened, was Shane.

"Dan!" Shane yelled.

"Don't worry, Shane," Daniel yelled back. "We're gonna get you out!"

"Slide the swords over to me," Hellfire said. "Then I will release him. Try to come over here and he dies."

"How do we know that you'll give him back once we've given you the swords?" Jake asked.

"You don't," Hellfire said, grinning. "But you can be sure that if you don't give me the swords he will die right here. After all, I killed my own brother; I will certainly not hesitate to kill yours."

"Your brother?" Gabe asked.

"Bradley," Hellfire answered. "Though you knew him as Hornet."

"He was your brother?" Robert asked.

"My weak, pathetic younger brother," Hellfire answered. "He has served me much better in death than he ever did in life. He gave me the orange sword. But that does not concern you! Slide the swords over now!"

"If he doesn't give Shane back we can always call out the Soul Sword," Daniel whispered.

Daniel and Jake bent down and slid the swords toward Hellfire. Daniel was back in his running clothes, and Jake was wearing shorts and a T-shirt. Both swords stopped right in front of Hellfire. He chuckled a bit as he bent down and picked up the blue sword. He touched the dark blue gem to the ones on his sword. The swords combined in a bright flash.

Hellfire picked up the green sword, touching the dark green gem to the dark ones on his sword. They then saw a sight that had been seen only once, nearly a thousand years earlier. They saw the same blinking that Ramsey had seen, and the same explosion of light. When Hellfire gripped the sword, the dark wave shot over him. The red spots on his armor changed to dark gray. He held the Shadow Sword in his trembling hand.

"All right, we kept our end of the deal," said Daniel. "Now you keep yours. Release my brother!"

"A deal is a deal," said Hellfire.

He walked over to the cage, and with one swipe of his sword, cut it open. Shane ran toward Daniel and the others, but Hellfire caught him by the back of the shirt. He placed the blade of the Shadow Sword along Shane's throat.

"On second thought, maybe I'd better keep him with me," Hellfire said. "Just in case you should try to awaken the Soul Sword. By the time you could get to it, he'd be dead anyway."

"How did you know about that?" Daniel asked. "Mercury said he didn't tell you about the Soul Sword."

"He didn't," Hellfire answered. "It wasn't too difficult to figure out the sorcerer's symbolism in the opposing gems, though. Then, when I found out the swords could be combined, I realized that ultimately the eight gems would become two opposing forces. Which is why I still need the young one. He is my only defense against your awakening the dormant force. He will be more than adequate in that role, I should think."

Hellfire laughed as he held Shane by the shirt in one hand and pointed the Shadow Sword at the other four boys with the other. Shane was struggling to pull away, but he couldn't. Hellfire was holding the shirt too tightly for Shane to move or slip out of it. Shane struggled, knowing that if he couldn't get away, they would all die. Each time he lunged forward, Hellfire pulled him back.

Shane lunged forward one final time, and Hellfire pulled him back again. This time, though, Shane used Hellfire's incredible strength to his advantage. He let Hellfire pull him, then turned and wrapped his arm around Hellfire's. He leaned all of his weight back, supported by Hellfire's arm. As he leaned back, he kicked up as hard as he could. He wasn't trying to hurt Hellfire; he knew he wasn't strong enough. He aimed, rather, for Hellfire's right hand, which held the sword. He kicked the handle of the sword and sent it flying right out of Hellfire's grasp. The Shadow Sword stuck into the ground in front of Hellfire.

Gabe and Daniel rushed forward as Hellfire changed back into his normal self. Shane turned and threw three fast punches into Hellfire's ribs. As Hellfire doubled over, Shane grabbed behind the villain's head and crashed a powerful knee into his foe's face. Hellfire jerked upright, and Gabe leapt in and threw a flying kick, which slammed into the villain's chest. Hellfire flew back, and Gabe and Shane ran back to Jake and Robert. Daniel grabbed the Shadow Sword, and pulled with all of his might.

He was not able to free the sword, no matter how hard he pulled. As Hellfire was recovering, Daniel pulled one last time, felt something release, and fell back. What he saw amazed him. He had not pulled the sword out of the ground; rather, he had pulled pure light out of the sword. The light was in the shape of a sword, and as he stood up it solidified into the Soul Sword. As the silver wave swept over him, his armor returned, silver where it had been green. He felt power course through him like he had never known.

"Dan!" exclaimed Shane.

"You OK, Shane?" Daniel asked.

"I ... I'm fine," Shane said, amazed at his brother's newest transformation.

"Good," Daniel said. "Now you all need to get out of here."

"We can't just leave you!" Gabe said.

"You have to," Daniel said, surprisingly calm.

"But we can help!" said Robert.

"Not this time," said Daniel. "I have to do this alone."

"Jake, say something to him!" Shane pleaded.

"Good luck, Dan," Jake said. "I know that if there is a way to survive, you'll find it."

"Tell everyone I love them very much," Daniel said. "And that I'm sorry things turned out this way. And tell them to throw a big party; I don't want anyone crying because of me!"

"Well, then, I guess we should be going," Gabe said. "Get in a good shot for me."

"Yeah, teach him a lesson for me!" said Robert.

"And make sure he knows that he can't kidnap me and get away with it!" Shane said.

"I will," said Daniel. "But you guys have to hurry; judging by what Mercury showed us of his battle I don't know if the cave will be able to take the force of ours. I command all four shields now; I will command them to obey you. They will take you to safety."

"Wait!" Shane shouted, running up to Daniel and hugging him. "You have to promise that no matter what, you won't die. Promise me!"

"I don't know if I can promise that," Daniel said, smiling at his littlest brother.

Gabe walked up, tears in his eyes, and hugged his older brother as well. Then he pulled Shane away.

"Take care of them, Jake," Daniel said.

"You know I will," Jake said. "I swear it."

The four shields went to the four boys. Jake jumped on the blue shield, Gabe on the red shield, Robert on the orange shield, and Shane on the green shield. With one final wave good-bye, Daniel watched them shoot off into the tunnel. Forcing the lump back down his throat, he turned to see Hellfire on his feet, the Shadow Sword already in his grasp.

"So you managed to awaken the other half," Hellfire said. "That's fine. You see I've been training for this moment, to finally face you again. And what a stage! This dome is our battlefield, but the world is our prize! I could not have imagined a grander ending than this."

"You attacked my friends and family," said Daniel, ignoring Hellfire's rant.

"Yes, that's right," Hellfire said. "And after I defeat you in the duel of duels, they will be the first ones to die!"

"You beat up Gabe, and kidnapped Shane," Daniel said.

"And I would do it all again to get my hands on this ultimate power!" Hellfire raised his sword into the air.

"I can't let your crimes go unpunished," said Daniel. "I can't let you hurt anyone else."

"You can't stop me!" Hellfire shouted. "I have trained for this specific moment: to destroy you!"

"You should never have brought my family and friends into this," said Daniel. "Now, no matter what, I cannot allow you to win."

"Don't be foolish," said Hellfire. "You will die down here."

"I have accepted that fate already," said Daniel. "I am prepared to die. But if I die, I'm taking you with me. Are you ready for that? Are you prepared to die?"

"I will not die, I will defeat you!" Hellfire shouted, taking a step back.

"You still don't understand, do you?" Daniel asked. "We both have to die. Our powers are exactly even. To restore peace to the world again, the vessels that contain this power must be destroyed, and the four must be restored. We will both die down here."

"I cannot be defeated!" Hellfire shouted.

"I am ready to die," said Daniel. "But no matter what, I cannot let you get away with what you've done!"

Daniel raised his sword up into the air and gripped it tightly. Then he dug his foot into the ground beneath him and pushed. He shot forward at Hellfire, his feet never touching the ground. As Hellfire blocked the slash, an enormous wave of energy shot from the two warriors. The walls shook, but they took no notice. Hellfire struggled to keep back Daniel's blade. As he did, Daniel threw a punch with his left hand that sent Hellfire flying back into the wall. Once again the walls shook from the power.

Hellfire struck back immediately. He put both feet against the wall and pushed, firing himself like a torpedo at the Silver Knight. He hit Daniel in the chest with both fists, then twisted and kicked Daniel in the same spot. Daniel fell to the floor, just managing to roll out of the way as the Shadow Sword came down to meet him. The walls shook with every movement.

He and Hellfire were both pushing themselves to their limits and beyond. As the fight raged on, they moved at such incredible speeds that normal people would not have been able to tell that a fight was taking place in front of them. To the warriors, it seemed like hours had passed, when in fact it was only a couple of minutes. Each second had slowed itself down just for their battle. Daniel kicked Hellfire and sent him flying backward. As he flew by his throne, the shockwave made it crumble and turn to dust. The walls shook and began to crack at the power of the battle. Water started to fill the bottom of the dome. Miraculously, the dome held.

The tunnel, however, was not doing nearly as well as the walls. It was quaking and crumbling, sending bits of rock down onto the riders. They did their best to dodge these new obstacles, as well as the ones already in their way. In the tight tunnel, however, there wasn't much of anywhere to go. Jake just prayed that the tunnel would hold until they got out. He didn't realize that Daniel was praying the same exact thing.

Daniel knew that the tunnel was unstable, so he had been trying his hardest to hold back, but Hellfire's power was too great and his control too masterful for Daniel to hold anything back. So, against his will, he contributed to the power that was knocking down the tunnel. They jumped at each other, having long exchanges before hitting the ground. It was reminiscent of their first spectacular aerial battle. Then Daniel launched one incredible final move.

He ran at Hellfire, planting his foot as hard as he could into the ground, and flying high over Hellfire's head. Hellfire jumped up to meet him, but found the Soul Sword striking down at his face. Daniel used the force of Hellfire's block to roll himself over his enemy's arm, and kicked him in the back. As Hellfire fell forward, Daniel rotated and grabbed his feet, then threw him up into the ceiling of the dome.

As he fell, Daniel fell with him, sending a barrage of punches and kicks at the stunned Hellfire. They rotated in the air, and when Daniel was above Hellfire he threw both feet down into Hellfire's stomach. This sent them crashing into the ground, with Hellfire screaming in pain. Then Daniel jumped, flipped, and faced Hellfire from across the room. For a second, Daniel though that he might have won, and survived the battle.

Then he noticed Hellfire struggling to his feet. He raised the gray gem to his face and said, "This is it. He has proven himself a powerful adversary, but I cannot let him win. I am the Shadow Warrior! I should rule the world! Help me take one last slash at him, and wipe him from this earth! We can do it; together we can wipe good from this earth forever! The world will be covered in shadow … our Shadow!"

The Shadow Sword began to glow a dark, menacing gray. It pulsed stronger and stronger as it readied itself for the final attack. Daniel raised the silver gem to his face.

"If I must die, I must," he said. "His evil cannot be allowed to continue. If we do not defeat him, no one will be able to stop him. He will take over the world. That is something I cannot accept. So let's do this, let's end it right here. For my brothers! For my friends! For my family! For Jamie! And for all the other innocent people all over the world!"

The Soul Sword glowed brightly, filling the room with its radiance. As the two swords glowed their fiercest, their holders rushed at each other, drawn together like magnets. The holders and the swords, together, rushed toward their destiny. Their battle cries could be heard through the tunnel, and out onto the beach on the other end. Their clash had all the brilliance and horror of an atomic blast. The bright light filled the dome, the tunnel, and the sky; a deafening roar echoed for miles. When the light cleared, the battle was over. Daniel stood over Hellfire, who was alive but down.

"Give up your sword," said Daniel.

"I don't understand," said Hellfire. "You aren't supposed to be better than me. We're supposed to be even!"

"The two swords are even," Daniel said. "We're not. You've been training for this for a month. I've been training for this my whole life. My whole life has been about pushing myself past my limits, becoming a better martial artist, and through that I've become a better human being. You've always relied on your brute force, but brute force doesn't always win. Because our powers were equal, it came down to who was actually a better fighter. In this case, it was me. Now give up your sword!"

Hellfire slowly reached up to give Daniel the Shadow Sword, but at that moment something happened. The final clash had shaken the tunnel enough to cause it to collapse. Jake and the others were just reaching the exit when the ceiling came down around them. Daniel turned his head in a panic, struggling to see what had happened at the entrance to the tunnel. Hellfire saw his opportunity, and quickly knocked the Soul

Sword from Daniel's hand. He stood up, sent Daniel flying across the room with a hard punch, and grasped both swords.

Daniel, back in his running clothes, could only watch in horror. Hellfire had one sword in each hand, with the gems facing each other. Then, with a fierce grin, he slammed the two gems together. The silver gem cracked and shattered, never to be formed again. The Soul Sword pulsed, turned back into its pure light form, and was sucked into the dark gray gem.

The gray gem glowed, and then turned black. At the same time, another black gem appeared on the other side of the sword. The sword itself shook as though it were in pain. The blade grew longer and twisted. The handle turned black and grew longer as well. Hellfire, in awe, grabbed the sword, and then screamed in agony as he himself changed.

First he started to grow until he was almost seven feet tall. His muscles bulged and grew to five times their former size. The armor faded from his torso and his skin became dry and cracked. It turned the same color that his original red armor had been. His hair disappeared as the skin on his face changed in the same way. Finally the mask across his eyes disappeared. One that covered his nose and mouth appeared, with points that extended past his ears. His voice was deep and thunderous as he spoke.

"You were right," he said. "We most certainly are not even! Now, finally, you will pay for each time you have humiliated me!"

Daniel found no words as the giant demon waited for a reply. Hellfire chuckled when he saw that Daniel could not speak. Even his laugh was demonic and frightening: no longer human. Whatever tiny bit of humanity and compassion Hellfire had had was now gone. The evil in his heart had completely conquered the good, and now Daniel was up against not only the most powerful being of all time, but a monster with no human kindness.

Daniel could not see Hellfire move until it was too late. He suddenly felt a burning sensation in his chest. He looked down to see that Hellfire had slashed him, though not deep enough to do any real damage. He soon felt the same pain in his back, across his cheek, his forehead, and down in his stomach. Hellfire had slashed him five times, never deep enough to kill him, but enough to make Daniel understand that he had lost.

Daniel fell to his knees in the middle of the dome. Hellfire was in front of him, standing where his throne had been. The demon's deep laugh shot straight through the wound in Daniel's chest. Suddenly Hellfire gripped the handle of his sword with two hands. The black gems began to glow with a dark, ominous light. What seemed like black lightning came from the gems and began to wrap around the sword, coiling up to the point. When the two streaks reached the tip of the sword they wound together. Hellfire threw his hands forward and a bolt of black lightning shot from the sword. It exploded into the ground right in front of Daniel, sending him flying back into the wall.

He shouldn't have missed, thought Daniel. *I should have been dead by now. He's toying with me, torturing me before he kills me.*

Another strike blasted through the wall next to his head, and the water began to pour in, threatening to drown him. As he fell, a strike exploded in front of him, knocking him back to his feet. The water quickly saturated the ground and started to rise. It was sloshing in his running sneakers as another strike tore through yet another part of the wall.

"Are you crazy?" Daniel shouted. "You'll bring the whole place down! We'll both die!"

"The power of the sword will save me!" Hellfire shouted back as he unleashed another black lightning strike.

Daniel hated the fact that Hellfire was toying with him. It brought back the fighting instinct in him. He had given up, but now he refused to die without at least trying to stay alive. He noticed that he was near the lowest of the platforms, so he jumped onto it. As he jumped to the next platform, the first one was destroyed by a black lightning strike. Daniel continued to go from platform to platform, but each time he reached a platform Hellfire was right behind him. The blasts were going through every part of the wall now, and the water was rushing in quickly. Daniel realized that the longer it took for the blasts to charge, the more powerful the blast would be, and the faster the dome would be destroyed.

Before long Daniel found himself on the third to last platform. He was about to jump when he looked up and saw Hellfire on the second to last one, right across from him. As Hellfire got ready to unleash a blast, Daniel looked up at the final platform directly above him. He jumped with all of his might as the blast destroyed his platform. He caught the top one with the tips of his fingers, and pulled himself up.

"Well, it's been fun," said Hellfire. "But now I'm afraid your time is up. I've got bigger and better things to do."

Daniel realized that he had nowhere to go, that it was finally over. He fell to one knee. Mercury, watching from the beach, saw the scene that he had envisioned so many times before, and closed his eyes, hoping that it would stop the visions from coming. Hellfire began to charge up his most powerful blast yet. He laughed as he charged it up, knowing that victory was his. For Daniel all of the noise of the dome went away. He couldn't hear Hellfire's maniacal laughter, or the water rushing in. He only heard his own breathing. He knew his time had come, that he had lost.

"I guess I'm no hero, after all," he said to himself, and hung his head.

Then he heard Mercury's voice, though not as usual. It was Mercury from earlier, right by his house. "The sword chose you because you *are* a hero," Mercury had said.

Then he heard his mother's voice from long before. "Of course it's the biggest you've ever faced. Otherwise it wouldn't be much of a challenge at all."

Next came his father's voice from just as long before. "I know you're afraid. It's OK to be afraid. Just don't let a little fear keep you from doing something extraordinary."

"But I can't do it," Daniel said out loud. "I'm no match for him, not alone. I'm not powerful enough."

In response he heard his own voice, from long ago. "True power comes from the heart."

He looked up to see Jamie, Liz, Ryan, and Jeanne cheering him on. Next to them he saw Gabe, Shane, Jake, and Robert, begging him to get up. Behind them he saw his whole family: aunts, uncles, cousins and grandparents. His friends from the dojo were right there with them, his sensei in front. They were all cheering him on, willing him to succeed. He could feel their energy flowing through him.

Next he heard Jamie's voice. "It doesn't have to be about saving the whole world. Maybe it is just about saving the people that you love," she had said.

Finally he heard Jake's voice, coming to him through the past from their first day in Paris. "You're never alone. Even when you're by yourself."

Daniel rose to his feet, filled with a new courage and a new energy. He could feel all of his loved ones behind him; he could feel their energy running through him. Just like in training, the people he cared about were giving him the energy he needed to succeed. The dark sword was powerful, but their love for him and his love for them was even more powerful. With them at his side, with them behind him, he knew that he could do anything. He couldn't give up, because they believed in him.

He saw that Hellfire's blast was almost ready, and he jumped. He did not jump at Hellfire, but away from him. He grabbed one of the metal chains that were still hanging from the ceiling, though it was not attached to a platform anymore. His momentum took him to the wall, and he pushed off hard. Hellfire unleashed the blast, but Daniel was already swinging. His angle pushed him around the blast, and then brought him straight back at Hellfire.

With the force of all of his loved ones behind him, Daniel put both of his feet forward. He struck the demon in the side. Hellfire was caught off balance, still unleashing the monstrous black lightning strike. The demon was knocked off of the platform and into the wall. The sword flew up and stuck into the ceiling as Hellfire fell forward. He barely caught the edge of the platform with one hand as he fell. Daniel could see that he was a normal person again, with normal clothes, and normal human fear in his eyes. He reached down and grabbed Hellfire's hand.

"Come on, we have to find a way out of here," he said, struggling to pull Hellfire up.

Hellfire looked Daniel right in the eyes and said, "My only consolation is that I die knowing you'll die, too."

With that he wrenched his hand loose and fell. Daniel tried to grab him, but he could not. He was staring Hellfire right in the eyes as he fell, and could see the fear and despair of a broken man. He looked away, unable to bear the sight. The water rushed in as the dome crumbled around him.

Chapter 12

Walking Away

Jake and the others made it out just in time, without so much as a scratch. When they reached the beach, they saw Mercury staring at the sound. Shane was the first to jump off his shield and join him, staring in vain over the water. Even though they could not see anything, it made them feel better to try.

"We shouldn't have left him," Gabe said, walking up.

"There was nothing we could have done," said Jake.

"There must have been some way we could have helped," said Robert.

"Yeah, there must have been something we could have done," said Shane. "He wouldn't have left us."

"No," Mercury said. "You four needed to be safe, so that he was not distracted."

Suddenly they heard a bloodcurdling scream and saw a pulse of energy sweep across the sound. They had no idea what, or who, it was, but Mercury could tell that it was Hellfire's scream as he changed into the demon, and the pulse of power was from the dark sword. They heard many ensuing explosions, and only Mercury knew for sure what was happening. The next couple of seconds seemed like hours for them, being so close to Daniel, and yet so far away. They were completely unable to help in any way, and it was eating them up inside. Even Mercury wished he could change the horrible future that he knew was coming.

Then they could see, in the middle of the sound, a great whirlpool. The water was filling the space as the dome crumbled, creating enough movement for them to see through the dark night. This went on for nearly a minute, and then all was still. The white water they had seen had once again become as dark and unmoving as the night sky. The tunnel had been destroyed, and the dome was now no more than a memory at the bottom of the Long Island Sound. And, to make matters much worse, there was no sign of Daniel.

"Where is he?" Shane asked tentatively.

"He's gone," Mercury said, hanging his head. "I'm sorry."

"You're sorry?" Gabe asked. "That's it? You're sorry? Well, sorry won't cut it! He's still alive, I know it! Use some of your sorcery, do something! You can't just let him die!"

"He is gone, Gabriel," Mercury responded. "And there is nothing that I can do. Even I cannot bring people back from the dead."

"I knew we should have stayed," Robert said.

"Then you would be dead as well," the sorcerer replied softly.

"That would be better than this," Jake muttered.

"It would be better than knowing we just let him die!" Gabe shouted.

"Your brother sacrificed himself so that you could survive," Mercury responded, sounding very calm. "We honor and regret the loss, but he served a greater purpose. You should be proud of him; he defeated the demon and saved the world! Now, together, the four of you will become earth's protectors."

"What do you mean?" Shane asked through tears.

"There are four swords, and four of you," Mercury said. "We will recover the swords from the bottom of the sound, and you will be entrusted with them. Jake, you will have the blue sword; Robert will take the orange sword. Gabe, you can have the red sword. And Shane, you can take over for your brother as the Green Knight, wielding the green sword. Together you four will fight for the ideals that Daniel died protecting."

"No, I don't want to," said Shane, falling down on the beach in tears. "I don't want a sword; all I want is my brother back!"

"I know how you feel," Mercury said.

"The hell you do!" Jake shouted back. "This whole thing has just been your game! You knew Dan was going to die, and you did nothing to stop it!"

"Yes, that's true," said Mercury. "If I had done something to stop it, then maybe Hellfire might be alive now, too. Then who knows what could have happened? This is the way it had to be! Daniel knowingly sacrificed himself so that you could survive and continue the struggle. And just because I know the future doesn't make it easier. It made it harder, because I've had to suffer this loss every day for the last thousand years! The swords are back at peace, and the world is safe. I know it is small consolation, but that is destiny."

"Who knew that destiny could hurt so much?" Robert moaned.

"Now we should go," Mercury said. "We will recover the swords tomorrow. For now we should get you home. We should honor his last wishes, and get you all home safely."

Jake and Robert hung their heads, saying nothing. Shane broke down in tears, not knowing how to accept his brother's death. Gabe cried, too, putting his hands on Shane's shoulders, trying to comfort him in some way: trying to do what Daniel would have done in that situation. They all knew that Daniel was a hero, and that he knowingly gave his life, but that did not make it any easier for them. They each, in their own way, blamed themselves for his death. In time, Mercury knew, they would come to understand this night, and how necessary it had been for all of them, and for all the people of the world.

Gabe helped Shane to his feet, and they all finally started to walk away, accepting Daniel's fate. The incredible emptiness they had inside would be a long time in filling, they all knew. But they also knew that moving on was the only way. They would always remember Daniel, and how incredibly heroic he was. Without knowing it, he had made them all better people. Jake, Robert, and Gabe jumped on their shields, and waited for Shane. Shane prepared to jump, but instead ran down to the edge of the water again.

"NO!" he shouted. "He's alive, I know he is! DAN! WHERE ARE YOU? DAN!"

Gabe walked over and put his hands on Shane's shoulders. "It's time to go," he said, and Shane could see that he was crying, too. "Dan isn't coming back."

Then, suddenly, they both noticed something strange about the water. The moon had two reflections. They rubbed their eyes, unable to believe the sight, but the moon definitely had two reflections. One was brighter than the other and *right over the spot where the dome had been*. It became brighter and larger as they watched, as though the moon were falling from the sky. Then they realized that the light was actually coming from underneath the water, surfacing slowly. When it was fully out of the water it looked like a bright ball of white light. It was so bright that they had to look away.

The light came to the beach, right in front of where they stood, and then touched down on the sand. As it hit the sand, the light disappeared, and they saw that the light source was actually a person, one with a very familiar face.

"Dan!" they all shouted at the same time.

It was Daniel, though he had changed quite a bit since they had last seen him. His armor looked the same, except that it was now white where it had been silver. The mask on his face was gone. His hair had turned completely white, and was standing straight up. Even his eyebrows were bright white. He had a brilliant white aura about him. Across his back was a new sword, with one white gem on either side. He was not wet, even though he had been under water, and all of his wounds had been healed. As he walked forward, he left no footprints in the sand.

"Dan, is that you?" Gabe asked.

"Yes," Daniel said, his voice echoing with a deep, warm resonance. "Sorry if I scared you."

"Are you a g … ghost?" Shane stammered.

"No," Daniel said, smiling. "I'm very much alive."

"And Hellfire?" Robert asked.

"He is gone," Daniel replied, dropping his head.

"So what happened in there?" Jake asked, in awe of his friend's new form.

Daniel told them everything that happened after they had left. "The dark sword was shaken loose as the dome crumbled. I knew that it was my only hope, so I dove after it. I caught it just inches from the ground, and then it transformed into this, and I was able to save myself. Sorry I took so long in surfacing, but this power is almost too much for my body to hold; I didn't want to push it."

"We almost left," Gabe said.

"I don't blame you," Daniel said. "Had I died, that's what I would have wanted."

"It was so horrible thinking you were dead," Shane said, hugging the White Knight.

The others did the same, hugging Daniel with tears of joy in their eyes. He found himself teary-eyed as well, remembering that it was only with their help that he was able to defeat the demon and save the world, and himself.

"Why couldn't I see this?" asked Mercury.

"Your job was done," said Daniel. "You no longer needed to guide the swords. You could only see the future of the swords until Hellfire was defeated because after that they had found their places. And because you could not believe that I would find a way to survive, you could not see it. Besides, you forgot that our future is what we make it. We humans control our own destinies. A thousand years of the same vision must have made you forget that."

"Yes, that is probably true," Mercury said, smiling. "Well, it now seems that you have some options."

"Which are?" asked Jake.

"Well, the first option is to get rid of the swords, leaving them on the bottom of the sound," Mercury said. "You will not be burdened with them anymore, but then I do not know who will find them. But Jake, that means that you can go off to the Marines."

"No, thanks," said Jake, smiling. "I'm sticking around here. I mean, what would these guys do without me? And besides, there's always going to be another enemy to fight."

"Good, I was hoping that you would say that," Mercury said. "Your next option is that Daniel can keep the white sword, and fight the forces of evil by himself."

"No," said Daniel. "I didn't get here by myself; I'm not going on alone. I'm better with their help anyway. I choose to be part of a team, this team."

"Very well," Mercury said. "Well, then, you know what to do, Daniel."

Daniel removed the white sword from its scabbard, and said, "Jake, I give you the blue sword, Gabe the red, Robert the orange, and I'll keep the green one for me."

He stuck the white sword into the ground, and released it. It glowed, and then separated into the four swords. Each sword was in front of its new holder, and they all reached out and grabbed their new weapons. The air was filled with color. They stood next to each other, their armor glowing with their bright colors. Shane smiled at the sight, but he was a little disappointed. He had given up his sword because Daniel was alive, but he now knew that he could never be a Knight.

"And what reward can I give to you?" Mercury said, turning to Shane. "You may be smaller, but tonight you proved yourself to be just as much a hero as any of the others. So what do you want?"

"I don't need a reward," Shane said, smiling.

"Which is exactly why you deserve one," Mercury explained.

The sorcerer raised his hands, and a pale blue light shot from them. Then a small sword appeared on a yellow shield, with yellow gems attached to it. Shane grabbed the hilt, and a yellow wave shot through the air. When the wave cleared, Shane stood in armor like the others, black streaked with bright yellow. The first yellow Knight.

"Isn't his sword small?" Robert asked.

"It will grow as he grows," Mercury responded.

"Congratulations," Daniel said. "And welcome to the team, all of you."

"Yeah, glad to have you with us," Jake said.

"Now we can really start helping," said Gabe.

"Now, do you notice something interesting about your swords?" Mercury asked.

"The dark gems are gone," Gabe said.

"Exactly," Mercury said. "When Daniel defeated Hellfire, he defeated the dark nature in the swords. You are now in control of the full power."

"Good job, Dan," Robert said.

"Thanks. And now I know why Hellfire and Hornet got the swords," said Daniel. "Gabe and Robert weren't going to Rome any time soon. And there needed to be a way for me to conquer the dark halves."

"It would seem so," Mercury said. "I'm glad that things worked out."

"What about you?" Jake asked. "What do you do now?"

"Well, I still have some more work to do around here," Mercury answered, "so I think that I will stick around a while."

"All right, sounds good," said Daniel. "You can help us learn to use our new power. But for now let's just go home and get some rest."

"Who's going to tell Mom that Shane is fighting with us?" Gabe asked.

"I say Mercury," Robert said.

"Wait, why me?" Mercury protested.

"She can't kill you," Jake said. "You're already dead!"

"Ah, good point," Mercury said with a chuckle.

The five boys jumped on their shields and headed for home. Mercury went along with them, hovering next to them as they flew. What adventures lay ahead for them even he didn't know. But they knew that no matter what, they would be able to overcome any obstacles, because they would face them together.